SNOWMAN SNOWMAN

Also by Janet Frame

Novels

Stories and Sketches

Poetry

Autobiography

SNO

VMAN SNOWMAN

FABLES AND FANTASIES
JANET FRAME

GEORGE BRAZILLER • NEW YORK

The story "The Red-Currant Bush, the Black-Currant Bush, the Gooseberry Bush, the African Thorn Hedge, and the Garden Gate Who Was Once the Head of an Iron Bedstead" appeared originally in Mademoiselle Magazine.

to John

CONTENTS

snowman snowman

1.

People live on earth, and animals and birds; and fish live in
the sea, but we do not defeat the sea, for we are driven back
to the sky, or we stay, and become what we have tried to
conquer, remembering nothing except our new flowing in
and out, in and out, sighing for one place, drawn to another,
wild with promises to white birds and bright red fish and
beaches abandoned then longed for.

I never conquered the sea. I flew at midnight to the earth,
and in the morning I was made into a human shape of snow.

"Snowman, Snowman," my creator said.

Two sharp pieces of coal, fragments of old pine forest,
were thrust in my face to be used for my eyes. A row of

brass buttons was arranged down my belly to give me dignity and hints of fastenings. A hat was put on my head, a pipe in my mouth.

Man is indeed simplicity, I thought. Coal, brass, cloth, wood—I never dreamed.

A passing bird, a half-starved gray sparrow said to me, "You are in prison."

But that was not so, it is not so now. I helped to conquer the earth, but because I did not arrive here with the advance armies, I have never seen the earth except in this whiteness and softness, and although I remember a time when I was not a snowman, the habit of being a man, a creature of coal, brass, cloth, wood, has begun to persist; yet it does not seem to have deprived me of my freedom. Even in the few moments after I was born I knew how to live, and for me it is easy, it is staying in the same place without any more flying, without trespassing or falling over cliffs or being swept down to sea and swallowed by the waves; never diving or dancing; staying the same, never influenced by change as human beings are; not having to contend with the invasions of growth which perform upon human beings in the name of time and change all the eccentric acts of whitening strands of hair, shrinking pink skin to yellow leather over bones gone porous, riddled with early-nesting sleep, stopping the ears, making final settlement concerning their quota of tumult; at last bandaging the eyes injured with seeing. Partly snow, partly man, I am preserved, made safe against death, by my inheritance of snow, and this I learned from the Perpetual Snowflake on the window sill.

Let me explain. It is the window sill of the house of the Dincer family—Harry, his wife Kath, and their daughter Rosemary. I belong to them. I stand forever now in their suburban front garden looking out upon the street of the city. Rosemary created me. I have learned something of her life from the Perpetual Snowflake who has explained to me the view, the situation, the prospect of my immortality and its relation to the swiftly vanishing lives of people.

I have a strange sensation of being, a mass chill and clumsiness, a gazing through pine-forest eyes upon a white world of trees drooping with snow, the wind stirring milk-white clots and curds of my essence in street and garden, for my immortality does not mean that I contain myself within myself, I breathe my essence in a white smoke from my body and the wind carries it away to mingle it with the other flakes of the lost armies that flew with me to earth, and that still fall—see them paratrooping in clouds of silk—but they do not recognize me, they float by without acknowledging my snowman-being rooted here in the white world with my limbs half-formed by the caprice and modesty of my creator who can scarcely know the true attributes of a man, who chooses coal, buttons, hat, pipe, as his sole fuel weapon and shroud.

Am I common property? On my first day, although Rosemary Dincer made me to stand in her front garden, people in the street kept pointing to me and saying to each other, "Look, a snowman, a snowman."

Children came in the gate and touched me or struck me or threw stones at me, as if I belonged to them. One man looking over the hedge at me remarked, "You won't be standing there so proudly for very long. Look at the sky!"

I looked at the sky and I felt lonely at the sight of the white whirlpool of the still-conquering armies, and I wondered if there were other snowmen, or do we exist singly and what is it that prompts people to make us?

Even Rosemary's making of me had caused her father to utter the strange observation, "A snowman at your age! Surely not!" which called forth the reply from his wife, Rosemary's mother, "Why not? It is not only children who make snowmen, anyone who has the chance makes a snowman, all up and down the town people are making snowmen!"

Why?

"Your time is limited, Snowman," someone remarked, looking over the hedge at me.

"How do you like your first day on earth, Snowman? Do you feel at home? Are you learning to see with those coal-black pine-forest eyes?"

That is the Perpetual Snowflake with his questions.

"Of course I can see. Everything is outlined clearly against the snow—trees, this tree beside me in the garden, the street, cars, people, buildings, everything is whole and contained within itself. The world is a remarkable place."

"I doubt if you will ever learn to see, Snowman. Trees, cars, streets, people, they are but the dark print upon the white page of snow. Your coal-black pine-forest eyes are no use until you are able to read the page itself, as men read books, passing beyond the visible obstructions of print to draw forth the invisible words with the warmth of their passionate breathing."

"But my breath is ice. And I am the white page. I have no passion. Is that why I shall live forever?"

He does not answer. Perhaps he is asleep.

Two doors away a little boy began to gather the snow to mold it into the shape of a man, but he grew tired of making a snowman, with the result that he abandoned it, and it stood half-formed, eyeless, faceless, with none of the salient emblems of humanity. A few moments later the child's father appeared with a tin of rubbish, last week's relics of Christmas—paper wrappings, tinsel, discarded angels, which he emptied over the body of the snowman, and drawing matches from a box in his pocket, he lit a fire, he made a fire of the neglected snowman, and from where I stood I could see the flames rising from the snow and a smoke or mist blurring the garden, and for an age I stared with horror at the flames and I could not turn my coal-black pine-forest eyes away from them, and even from where I stood safe in the Dincer garden I could feel my cheeks burning as if they sought to attract the fire. Soon the half-formed snowman disappeared and the tinsel, the paper wrappings, the discarded angels, were transformed to black ash. I sensed an assault on my own being, but I could not discover traces of it though my cheeks were wet not with tears of rage or sadness but with a stealthy nothingness of wet as if in some way I were being drained of my life, and I knew although I could not seem to make the effort to consider the significance of it, that fire was my enemy, and that should fire flow or march against me in its crimson ranks of flame I should be helpless and without courage and my urge to escape would lead only to my swifter dissolution.

"Your first day on earth and already you consider death?"

"Oh no, oh no."

My confidence returned. Oh the ease, the simplicity of static living! What wonders I observe with my coal-black pine-forest eyes! Is it not taken for granted that I shall live forever?

"Snowman, Snowman, a germ cell like a great sleeping beast lies curled upon the Dincer doorstep, tethered to past centuries, and every time Harry Dincer comes staggering up from the King's Arms he trips over the lead of the sleeping beast. Harry is a telephonist. He saw an advertisement in the daily paper, a picture of a man wearing headphones, listening to the world in conversation. ' 'Ullo Marseilles, Paris, Rome,' the man was saying, and Harry was filled with a desire for a similar chance to eavesdrop on the world's conversations, therefore he became a telephonist; but they have never put him on the Continental Circuit. He cannot speak the languages.

"So he goes to the King's Arms and gets drunk and staggers over the lead of the sleeping beast."

"I can see nothing on the front doorstep but a small mat for wiping feet, and yesterday's footprints dark with mud and soot."

"You will understand, Snowman. Tomorrow and the next day it will be clear to you.

"It is a matter of age. Of sickness, accident, time, of the assaults people make one upon the other. They are organized and trained to kill because the growth of centuries has entangled them in the habit as in a noxious weed which they are afraid to eradicate because in clearing the confusion between being and being, the thick hate-oozing stems, the blossoms feeding upon the night-flying jealousies and hungers, they face each other set in an unbearable clearing of light and proper original shade, with the sky naked in its truth, and what protection is there for them now as they crouch in fear of the new light, with none of them brave enough to stand tall, to welcome the eradication of death? Or they kill on impulse because, loving too much, they isolate the act of love and thus extend it to encompass the memorable loneliness of death; they choose to make one visit to the altar of possession, imagining that wherever and whenever they return, the scene will be unchanged. They find it has vanished, Snowman, as soon as the killing is over. And the stained glass is not pictures in beautiful compartments of color: it is blood.

"You will understand, Snowman. Tomorrow and the next day it may be clear to you. You will learn part of the meaning of the people who made you, of the street and the city. You will know that Harry Dincer is deeper and deeper in despair because he is unable to say ' 'Ullo Paris, Rome, Marseilles,' to communicate over thousands of miles in a foreign tongue, that although he is a telephonist with his own headphones more select and private than ears, he will never be given permission to work on other than his allotted circuit. 'My headphones.' He brings them from work at night and polishes them. Has skin-to-skin conversation failed him so sadly? 'My headphones. I've heard famous people talking in private. Conductors of orchestras, stars of show business and television, so many stars I couldn't count them if I tried.' "

"We heard rumors of stars in the sky on our journey to earth. Are people stars?"

"You will understand, Snowman, tomorrow and the next day and the next day. You will know the child who made you, and her mother, and their house and their car, their gondola shopping bags, their television sets, all of which may seem to you, a snowman, to be irritating trivialities, but when you learn to consider them it will be of their deeper layers that you think. You will have noticed how buildings emerge from the earth—houses, the shops at the corner, plants, your neighbor tree that is burdened with snow. All these things—even televisions and gondola shopping bags, are anchored to the earth or to people upon the earth, and when you find the point of anchorage, the place which most resists the ravages of the tides of forgetfulness and change, there you will also find the true meaning of the objects, their roots, those hairy tentacles which embrace the hearts of people or merely cling there, like green moss to a neglected stone that no one will ever want to overturn to observe the quick-running life beneath it.

"Tomorrow and the next day you may understand."

"Is it necessary? I am only a snowman."

Who is the Perpetual Snowflake? I never knew him before though our family is Snowflake. On my first day on earth I have known pride, fear, curiosity, and now sadness for I cannot ever return to the lost fields of snow that are not on the earth, that have no houses no cities no people. I cannot go back to be among my sisters and brothers far in the sky, lying in our cold white nightclothes while a calm wind ties down the corners of the sky, arranging the covers of cloud over our white sleeping bodies. I have been made Man. I am an adventure in immortality. Is it not a privilege to be made Man?

It is night now. There is a golden glow from the street light stretching its golden beak across the white street. It says no word but a quiet humming sound issues from it, as a life-signal.

I close my coal-black pine-forest eyes and sleep.

2.

There is a clock in the city. It keeps time. That is remarkable, isn't it? When the snow came the clock stopped suddenly because the hands (which grasp) had frozen, and workmen climbed ladders to reach the clock's head, and they burned small fires day and night behind its face to warm it, with the result that it soon kept time once again. Time can be rejected, refused, or kept. The chief problem is where to keep it as there is not much space on earth for invisible property. It is easier for people to put shopping into gondola shopping bags than to put time into a convenient container.

I am worried. My back aches. I have a feeling of rigidity, my roots seem so far from my head, there is no communication between them as there was on my first day on earth when I could say to myself, My one foot is in place, and know that it was so. Now I do not seem to have control of my knowing, it has floated from me like the smoky breaths floating from the people in the street when they open their mouths. The Perpetual Snowflake has confused me by trying to explain the earth when I know there is nothing to explain. The earth is covered with snow. It has always been covered with snow.

I feel so strange. He has told me that people eat dead animals and that before they choose which part to eat they mark and map the carcasses in blue or red pencil, the latitude and longitude of death. The lines are joined. Everything is named and contained and controlled. Today I seem to feel like an animal that is being killed slowly, but I have not the certainty of knowing the boundaries and labels of my own body, and if I see red marks in the snow I expect they will be not red pencil but blood. I experience the same heaviness which overcame me yesterday shortly after I was born. My head sinks deep into my shoulders, my laughter is invisible and does not show on my face or in my eyes.

I frown.

I have a feeling of anxiety because no one has yet taken my photograph, yet it seemed a promised event of importance when I heard Kath Dincer say to her husband, "We'll take a photograph of it while it lasts. We must at all costs get a photo of the snowman!

Large gray drops of water are running down my face.

"Mummy, the snowman's crying!"

A child walks by with her mother. They are going shopping, around the corner to the greengrocer's. The little girl is tightly parceled in woollen clothing, bright red, with a cap fitting close to her head and brown boots zipped on her feet. Her face is rosy. She belongs to the snow, all the children belong to the snow, see them sliding, scuffing, throwing snowballs, hear them shouting with their voices leaving their mouths and forming into brilliant piercing icicles suspended in the clear air!

The children dance; their footmarks have the same delicacy as those of cats, dogs, birds.

I perceive that all children are the enemies of their elders, and that the snow possesses a quality which causes all pretense of love between them to be discarded.

"Mummy, the snowman's crying!"

The little girl points to my tears which are not tears.

"Stupid, he's not crying. He's only a snowman."

"But he's crying!"

"It's only snow, love."

"If I hit him will he cry?"

"Don't be silly. He'll fall to pieces."

Now that was strange. Would I fall to pieces?

"Come here won't you, I don't know what the snow does to you, you can't go into other people's gardens like that. The snowman doesn't belong to us."

"Who does the snow belong to, Mummy?"

"Don't be silly, love, I suppose it's everybody's."

"Then the snowman's ours!"

"Don't be silly, stupid, it belongs to the person who made him."

Everything is very confusing. Do I belong to Rosemary Dincer because she made me, and to Kath because Rosemary belongs to Kath and to Harry because Kath belongs to Harry, and who does Harry belong to, does belonging describe a circle which starts again at Rosemary or does it extend to all people and everybody belongs to everybody else on earth? Who decides?

"What is around the corner, and in the houses, and who are the people and how do they accommodate time when he is their guest?"

"Around the corner there is a gas main, a wood louse, an empty carton, a man's ear, a desolation, a happiness, shops and people."

"I mean what is there in its rightful order. Surely there are no ears lying on the pavement and no one is sweeping out a desolation with the night's dust from the floor of the grocer's!"

"Oh you want facts the usual way, as people arrange them through habit? You want a human focus? You prefer me to abolish the gas main and the empty carton and present the complete man instead of his Ferris wheel of a left ear; you wish to play parlor games like join the dots and name the important objects in the picture.

"It is what is known as a built-up area. With fifty square yards you have a population of hundreds. Now there are instruments to measure the sound of planes, cars and other machines, but not to measure the enormous sound of people living, their hearts beating, their digestions working or refusing to work, their throats being cleared to make way for mighty language, their joints creaking, bones grinding, hair, skin and fingernails growing, and the roller-coaster movement of their thoughts. Why, even the measurement of a man's heart beating is a wearisome business, with one person appointed as a special listener, and listening so solemnly to the wild echoes within. What hope is there of hearing a man's heart, recording the storms, the sudden darknesses and flashes of lightning, the commotions of unseen life? No one really listens to the beating of a heart. He merely listens to the listening of the stethoscope which in its turn has been eavesdropping and transmitting the most secret nameless sound which no one has ever heard distinctly, nor is anyone certain that the secret sound is not itself merely listening and transmitting another murmur which is yet more remote, and so on, to the center, the first sound that cannot be heard apart from that other insistent murmur like the inland sea. And to think that Harry Dincer lives in despair because he is not qualified to put on his polished headphones and get in touch with Paris, Rome, Marseilles!

"People live here in the street of the city, in a constant commotion. Their lives are bustled and stirred and tasted like a big Christmas pudding packed with cheap good-luck tokens, little bells and fairy shoes that look as if they are made of silver, but they feel too heavy in the hand and they are perhaps poisonous. Life here, Snowman, is a big dark mess. Of course you are only a snowman and do not need to take account of the lives of people. See that house on the corner? The people living there have such a struggle to persuade the postman to deliver the letters addressed there, for the house is neither in one street nor in the next, and the owners are always painting heavy black numbers on the gate, and the numbers get larger each time they are painted, for it is so important for people to know where they live, and to let others know, to have their places defined and numbered. The family who live in that house have a passion for looking alike and that is quite natural for it is a family, yet the likeness is so startling that if you look from either of the two sons to his father you have the confusing impression that your eyes have telescoped time, that your glance at the son has caused him to arrive in a twinkling at middle age, to abandon his career as an apprentice accountant or an industrial designer and become his father, the homeworker, sitting in the little top floor room under the neon strip light sewing men's trousers and overcoats, with the whirr-hum of the machine penetrating the house and the sounds from the radio, Music While You Work, coming through the open window into the street; always a noise of work, an occupational murmur; it is the modern fairy tale, Snowman, it is not the old grandmother who sits in the attic spinning, but the father, the homeworker, weaving spells into overcoats.

"It is also strange that if you glance from either of the sons to his mother you experience the same feeling of the concentration of time, with the son becoming his own mother, the mother being transferred to the son. The face of mother, father, sons, has each changed from an individual right and possession to a family concern. Instead of saying proudly of mother and son, 'Look, you can see the likeness,' you feel a sense of uneasiness, of the massing of hidden determined forces which will destroy every obstacle in order to retain their right-of-way within the deep genetic groove.

"This family has a new car. The two boys spend Sunday mornings inside the new car, with the hood up, studying it; or sitting in the driver's seat or the back seat; standing, looking, touching. Sometimes they drive slowly round the block followed by the three West Indian children from next door, dressed in their Sunday best, bunched and frilly as daffodils.

14

"You are startled, Snowman? Daffodils? There's nothing to fear, Snowman. I have my own story, you know. I cannot tell the length of time I have been away from the sky and it is months of years since snow fell like this, reaped summer wheat into lily-white flour and all the cars huddled in the streets, look, like barracuda loaves of bread without any crust, only crisp snow for tasting by the saw-toothed wind, oh Snowman you need not fear daffodils for they mean nothing these days, they are forced, compelled, the pressure is put on them. People stamp and trample on everything, including other people, and everything rises dazed, dazzling, complete, from the earth. And so round and round the block the boys go in the new car, and the children follow laughing and screaming with their black eyes shining. Oh no who need be afraid of daffodils?

Sunday morning is a separate season. In the afternoon the people watch television, that is except for the West Indian family who hold a Church Service in their upstairs rooms with their friends and relations coming from far and near, the women and children resplendent in brocades, flocked nylon, satin, the men in carefully pressed suits with bright shirts and polished shoes. They open all the windows of the room, the pianist begins to play, the congregation begins to sing, and you can hear the hymns even from where you are standing in this garden. They are not sung in a tone of weariness and complaint, as people sing when they are trying to catch up with God on the Grand March but are suffering from stones in their shoes and blisters on their feet: they are sung with gaiety and excitement as if God were outpaced, as if the congregation were arriving before him, to make everything comfortable with provisions and shelter in preparation for the long long night.

"At this time of year they sing carols: 'From the Eastern Mountains Pressing On They Come.' 'Away in a Manger.' 'Oh Little Town of Bethlehem.' The children from the Council Flats around the corner, the boys of twelve and thirteen set free on Sunday, with nowhere to go and nothing to do, stand outside the house, mimicking the singers, adopting special piercing voices, as they mimic everything, for boys of that age, Snowman, are not people at all, they make noises like engines and lions and airplanes whenever they pass in a gang along the street, all making the noise at once, interrupting it sometimes with fragments of human language which no one listens to, and do you know, Snowman, I can never understand how without talking to one another, with only animal, machine, engine cries and disturbances of sound, these boys can yet decide so unanimously where they are going, and they swagger along in the direction of the Park or the Green or their favorite café as if one of them had said clearly in human speech, 'We'll go here, eh?'

"On Sunday afternoons the man in the house opposite watches television. He comes from Barbados. He bought the house a few months ago and moved into the vacant flat on the ground floor, and at first whenever his student friends came to see him the white people occupying the top floor would lean from their wondow, popping back and forth like cuckoo clocks trying to arrange a regular rhythm. 'Blacks,' said the people on the top floor, and gave notice. Those on the second floor stayed. Myra, her husband Ken, their daughter Phyllis. People have names. Ken is short and muscular with his bones arranged firmly and squarely as if to support unusual or surprising turns and somersaults of flesh—like those steel jungle-gyms in children's playgrounds which are always crowded with children swinging on them and climbing and hanging from them, their knees gripping the bars, arms dangling, faces growing redder and redder.

"People passing say warningly to each other. 'Look at them. The blood will go to their head.' You see, when people grow up they learn to be afraid of what is happening inside their own bodies, and they become anxious and suspicious if their blood travels suddenly from here to there, or if their hearts, tired of staying in their accustomed places, quite naturally 'turn over'; and thus they are resentful of the way children seem so unconcerned when they dangle from jungle-gyms and their blood goes to their heads. Why? the adults wonder. Why can't they learn that blood going to the head is not a simple healthy matter like an impulsive excursion to the seaside?

"Myra is stout with dark hair and eyes and an ordinary face, as most faces are, with its lines and pouts and puckers and its tired middle-aged skin layered with Cake Makeup, Invisible Foundation, Fairy-Spun Face Powder. Every afternoon Myra dresses carefully and goes to the telephone box at the end of the street to make a call. To whom? I don't know, and Ken doesn't know. See the telephone box? The directory has H to K missing because last weekend some people known as *youths* tore pages from the directory and smashed the mirror on the wall and tried to wrench the telephone from its stand. People have such a hate and love for telephones. ' 'Ullo Paris, Rome, Marseilles. Hold the line a minute, I have got through to your heart. S.O.S. Save our Souls.'

"Snowman, I heard of a man who sent to a mail-order firm for a radio transmitting and receiving set. When he assembled the kit of tiny parts he found that he could send or receive only one message, S.O.S. He listened day and night, and he never found out who was sending the message or why he himself should be sending it, for he didn't need to ask for help, he was not in despair, not bankrupt or crossed in love; his life was happy.

"He got up one morning, washed, dressed, looked out of his window at the world and shot himself."

"I am sure it is interesting. But I am only a snowman."

"Phyllis is very thin. She wears mauve eyeshadow and mauve lipstick and the expression on her face implies that she can't understand or didn't hear clearly or interpret correctly the sound of the world about her. She works in a dusty cut-price store a threepenny bus ride away although while she was at Secondary Modern she dreamed of being a secretary, a receptionist, the manageress of a *boutique*. She spends her time amongst pieces of timber, wallpapers, paraffin cans, last year's boxed Christmas soap and cheap perfumes, dented dust-covered cans of Mulligatawny and Cream of Kidney Soup; pots, brooms, double toilet rolls; prices slashed. Even the sweets displayed in the opened boxes in the window beside the bathcubes and the plastic dishes and the free offer tube of toothpaste with shampoo riding strapped to its back, are all covered in dust. The licorice allsorts are shrunken and crippled with age.

"On Friday nights Phyllis goes with her Indian girlfriend to the pictures or the youth club, and on Fridays when the knocker downstairs is rattled and banged and Myra opens the living-room window to see who is visiting, she has to make her observations very carefully, for usually if she looks down and sees someone with dark skin she exclaims, 'Not for us! It's for upstairs or downstairs.'

"But on Friday nights when the young Indian girl comes for Phyllis, Myra has to make sure to let her in, but she finds it so difficult especially on these murky winter evenings to know whether the caller has Indian skin or West Indian skin or European skin, it seems all the same when the light has gone.

"A West-Indian woman and her husband live now on the top floor. He works as a conductor for London Transport. There is a new baby, Cynthia. For months the young woman, Gloria, sat up there at the window every day staring down at the street, only venturing outside to shop at the grocer's or the butcher's around the corner, and then she would walk slowly and carefully, leaning backwards, with her baby safe as a coconut inside her. Then suddenly two faces appeared one day at the window, that of Gloria and of a tiny baby in a white shawl, but Gloria withdrew the bundle quickly and did not let Cynthia see out of the window for many many weeks, as if she were preparing her by first explaining to her the curious ways of people in the world. And during that time Gloria did not go out, even to the grocer's or the butcher's, but stayed inside with Cynthia, and the curtains were drawn across the window, and one evening when Gloria's husband came home from issuing tickets on the one-seven-six Catford to Willesden, Willes-

den to Catford, he brought a bundle of lace which Gloria
made into curtains, and now there were two pairs of curtains
to protect Cynthia and her mother from the world, and
though it was summer with the world banging singing
screaming echoing and the voices and radios loud in the
street and the cars hooting and dogs barking and jet planes
shuddering the sky, there was no sound at all from the room
with the double curtains, and the window stayed shut, and
no faces looked out. The husband went to work in the
morning and came home at night. The district nurse called
sometimes, propping her bicycle against the fence, staying
ten or fifteen minutes in the house, then coming out, saying
nothing, going immediately to her bicycle, unlocking it,
putting her bag in the basket over the handle bars, cycling
down the road, disappearing round the corner, and who
knows if she did not then reach the edge of the world and
drop into darkness with the shining steel spokes of the back
wheel of her bicycle spinning blindly like a star?

"Suddenly one day the double curtains were drawn aside.
There were two faces at the window, Gloria, and her baby,
sitting up in the cot which had been moved to the window.
Gloria took the tiny black hand, held it high, and waved
it merrily at the world.

"Cynthia knew now, you see. All the while, in the secre-
tive room behind the double curtains, her mother had been
teaching her, preparing her, and now everything was arranged for Cynthia to consider the world outside. If you
look up there now, Snowman, you will see the baby's face
staring from the window. She still hasn't learned to wave by
herself, but she laughs and cries at what she sees, and this

20

morning with you here in the garden, and with the world all sheet and tablecloth and napkin, she cannot understand, she does not know that if she came outside to tread on the snowy tablecloth she would leave footprints in common with all other creatures living or dead who touch the snow: birds, cats, branches of trees, people, the old man with the shovel, the child with the stones and the snowballs, and Cynthia's own father on his way to work with the one-seven-six to Willesden."

It has begun to snow again. Reinforcements. I am feeling safe though my newest white coat obscures my sight. Children keep running into the garden and stealing from me— one has taken a brass button; or they prop me up with more snow as if I were in danger of falling. Sometimes they make strange menacing remarks about what will happen to me *after*. After what? Am I the only snowman in the world now?

"Others are appearing in the city. Perhaps they are your distant relations. Some are seven feet tall and others are only three feet tall. Some wear uniforms and carry weapons such as swords, umbrellas, sticks, newspapers. And all have been made by children or by those whom others regard as children. Living in the house by the telephone box there is a middle-aged woman who is four feet high and has the understanding of a child. She is employed to clean the house belonging to the Indian doctor and it is she who every morning polishes the brass plate outside his door and erases the rude remarks A Wog Lives Here, Go Home Black, with a drop of Cleanic upon a bright yellow cloth. It is marvelous, Snowman, the way Cleanic can remove all trace of an overnight scar; it ought to be more used by human beings when they suffer attacks from those who love them so much that they must write their love as insults upon the heart of the loved. Have human beings hearts of brass?

"Snowman, Snowman, after the woman whose real name is Dora but whom everybody calls Tiny, had polished away the insults, and had cleaned the surgery and the other rooms in the house and had shopped at the grocer's for her mother, and had walked home up the road, carrying her little bag of private possessions and family food, she went outside to the back garden of her home and made a snowman. She made him exactly her own size, to fit, eye level with eye, mouth with mouth and heart with heart. The two matched perfectly.

"Then as soon as she had finished making him she stared at him with her head on one side and a serious expression on her face. She decided to push him over and get rid of him. No. She decided to keep him there in the garden forever. So she laid a ring of pebbles around him as a sign that he belonged to her and that no one was to touch him, and she went inside to her lunch. In the afternoon on her way to work she stopped everyone she met and explained that she had made a snowman.

" 'I made a snowman. He's mine.'

"No one disputed that. Apparently if you make a snowman he belongs to you, and although children might pluck out his eyes and carry off his bright buttons and plunge his hat over his head so that he cannot see, no one will try to steal the whole snowman because he belongs to the person who made him.

"Later in the afternoon when Tiny returned from work she became angry with her snowman, at the way he stood in the garden, not speaking or smiling or moving, just submitting to the perpetual collision of fresh flakes upon his body. Tiny's anger increased. She began to cry, not simple crying with tears running down her cheeks but a moaning complaining cry without tears. Then seizing the garden shovel which had helped her to make her snowman, Tiny battered the snowman over the head, and his eyes fell out, his body broke in two, he sank within the charmed pebbled circle, making no protest, soundlessly. Tiny put away the shovel in its correct place in the garden shed and she went inside to watch television while she knitted the palm of the right hand of the gloves she is making to protect herself from the everlasting cold.

"Another of your relations was a three-inch-high snowman standing upon a cake in a shop window. He wore a red woolen cap, smoked a red pipe, and of course wore buttons, little red round ones placed in a row down his fat belly. I believe that he was different from your other relations because no one saw him being made and when people passed him they did not make the remarks which you find so fearful—about the day *after* or 'what will happen soon,' or 'let him wait a few days and he won't be so proud.' He was taken from the shop, shut in a dark box, carried to a strange room and placed in the center of a table laden with food. The room was hung with decorations, glittering trees and lights and angels, in fact it was such a dazzle that the snowman may have imagined that he had arrived in heaven except that the angel at the top of the tree gave him no welcoming smile, her face seemed made so that she could not smile, it was a face with a small split of red like a cut, while the lights twinkling round her gave her skin a yellow color blotched with shadow which made her two tiny black specks of eyes look like mouse dirt dropped in porridge, and that is no way for an angel to appear; therefore your distant relation couldn't have arrived in heaven, though it may have been a matter of opinion, as the people in the room were in the happiest mood, snatching kisses from one another, drinking sparkling wine, unwrapping presents given as a sign of their love. Snowman, it was a typical scene of human happiness.

"Now a snowman, though he is made of snow, is in some respects human. Imagine the feelings of a snowman when he observes that when people are in their happiest mood they are likely to seize and devour each other. I do not mean to make you afraid when I tell you that one of the guests walked over to the table, grasped your distant relation, and treating him as if he were an article of food, began to bite, chew and swallow him, while the party continued as if nothing unusual had happened. And later, when the rejoicing was over, the men took their women to bed and because they were again so happy they seized and devoured each other and the eating continued all night yet nobody disappeared like your poor three-inch-high snowman. It seems that people who have lived on the earth for so many centuries have used much of their cunning to discover this marvelously secret way of concealing the fact that they are continuously eating and being eaten by those whom they love."

Why should I be afraid? There are gray envelopes flapping in the sky and the trees are writing their destinations against the sky, and pinned to the corners of the clouds are the red-footed storks so eager to be flying south to sit upon a golden pyramid and sharpen their beaks on the golden stone. I remember this, though I am only a snowman. I like to look up at the sky. And then I look out at the street and think of what the Perpetual Snowflake has told me of the people, and I wonder to myself, Where are the heroes driving through the streets in their chariots? I thought the earth was filled with heroes, with happiness, and so it is, oh yes, I have a feeling of happiness, there's just a soft settling of new snow brushing my cheeks, and white fellow-snowflakes disguised as dragonflies tickling my nose, and a passing child has made two hands for me and enclosed them in furry red and yellow mittens. Each day I live someone adds to me or substracts from me, therefore perhaps I am more human than I realize? Then I must be happy, as human beings are, for in spite of the story of the three-inch-high snowman and the Christmas party, it cannot be true that people eat each other. They eat only vegetables and fruit and other animals who do not speak their language, and birds, and fish. People do not drink each other's blood. They drink wine, beer, milk, tea, coffee.

"Snowman, Snowman, there is a great gale of fear blowing in the snowflakes, for when it snows the earth is obscured and people are unaware of the divisions between street and pavement and they become afraid for they have always known where to walk. The obliteration of the earth enhances the need to touch it, to feel the shape of it, to be guided by it, knowing its hard and soft places, its corners, hollows, ravines, hills brushed by stars, valleys with lion-winds raging with their golden manes indistinguishable from the mountain grass, oh Snowman, all recognition has been wounded."

"I am only a snowman. I am surely and permanently anchored in a small suburban front garden. Here is Rosemary Dincer, my creator. I belong to her. Why is she crying?"

"She went to the Modern Jazz club where she met a University student on holiday who promised to ring her and make a date but when he rang her mother answered the phone and said, 'Do you know how old she is, she's only thirteen,' and he said, 'Oh. Tell her I'm sorry.' And that was the end."

"The end? Do people cry when it is the end?"

"People do not cry because it is the end. They cry because the end does not correspond with their imagination of it. Their first choice is always their own imagining; they refuse to be deterred by warnings; they say I choose this because although the price is high the thing itself is more precious, durable and beautiful. The light of imagined events is always so arranged that the customers do not see the flaws in what they have chosen to buy with their dreams. Rosemary bought so much happiness from her meeting with the University student and from the cinema date which followed, and then the concert, and then the excursion up the river, her visit to his home, his visit to her home. . . . Now it is the end."

"I thought the end was death. Is Rosemary dead?"

"Rosemary is not dead. There are other places where people may find the end: the edges of cliffs, the corners of streets, the lines of boundaries, the conjunctions of sentences, the disappearance—I should say the melting—of dreams. There is the view which suddenly comes to an end not because it is the end but because an obstacle stands or takes root there and will not be displaced. Rosemary's age is blocking the path of her dreaming. There are other powers which produce and arrange obstacles. Daylight, Time, Chance, Fear, the sudden closing of two blades of scissors, crocuses, a broken wall with grass growing through the cracks—like the wall over the road which the man who bought the house takes care to inspect each evening, peering into the joints of the brick for signs of decay. On his first morning as a tenant he heard two housewives talking outside: 'A colored man has bought this house. It will go to rack and ruin.'

"Rack and ruin, Snowman, is a sleepy quiescent stage before death; it allows waiting weeds and insects to nest and flourish, and the once solid bricks to move, shudder, breathe decay, split, crumble and fall.

"After one energetic day of troweling damp concrete into the crack in the brick the man gave up. He had grown wise. A woman passed him with her face going to rack and ruin and no amount of troweling could have hidden the decay. So why should he care what people were thinking? If some people thought of his race as a forerunner of death, well let them. It was flattering, in a way, for death is impersonal in these matters whether it is a question of the decay of a brick wall or of a human face."

"But snowmen do not decay? A fresh overnight fall of snow and we are new. Is Rosemary dying then?"

"It is a human habit to provide remedies for grief because even if tears are a common and usual sign of unhappiness they must never be allowed to become emissaries of death, to claim more than brief significance. 'Things' are the remedy most used by people to cure grief, disappointment, discomfort, celebration by tears and laughter, in order to return to a deathless Eden—a level uncluttered garden—vegetable state with drops of dew shining like mirrors between the separate lives, with the sun cradled in the leaves, the misty morning webs and traps making the air glimmer with deceiving lightness, with the earth safe and solid underfoot."

"Safe and solid underfoot?"

"You have never seen it that way, Snowman. Snow is a mass camouflage. No people would accept a government which performed the world-wide deceptions of snow; or perhaps they would be unable to resist the comfort of its beautiful treachery? I have seen the earth before and after snow. You may see it too when you become an old-fashioned Perpetual Snowflake talking to next year's old-fashioned snowman.

"But I was telling you of remedies. 'Things' are an effective and popular remedy. Most people begin using them very early in their lives. I don't know how it began and I'm not going to travel back until I reach the beginning, not simply for your sake, Snowman, for I may discover the real nature of the beginning, and that may frighten me, and you. Besides, I may not recognize it when I reach it, for the beginning like the end is never labeled. What should I do if I reached the beginning and thought that I had arrived at the end? What should I do? Both the beginning and the end demand such drastic action that I should be forced to decide immediately, and what if I made a mistake? There are responsibilities which even I am not prepared to face.

"Now Rosemary's life is full of things. A tape recorder, a piano, plenty of clothes—'winkle-picker shoes, a white raincoat, slacks, chunky jerseys; a duffle bag, a school case with her initials in gold upon it; a share in the family car, television, a caravan in Sussex. She is given pocket money each week. Next year she will go for a skiing holiday on the Continent. The difficulty of things or objects as remedies is that the supply of them depends upon income and that is not earned according to the tally of grief. There may be a time when there is no money left, and no more things, and no more remedies, and the tears will keep running down little girls' cheeks for ever and ever, or until the little girls grow up and trowel cement upon their faces to hide the rack and ruin.

"Tonight Harry and Kath will decide what to give Rosemary in order that she may be able to bear the disappointment of being too young. I myself do not know what happens inside people when they long for the companionship and adventure of another, and are given instead a box of chocolates with separate handmade centers, or a new dress or the top of the pops gramophone record. I suppose they get used to the comfort of things, and may even approach the state of holding a thrilling conversation with one of the handmade centers. Things are really much more convenient to human beings than their own kind; things can be thrown out when they are not wanted; they can be destroyed, torn to pieces or burned without questionings of conscience; the only effective way of destroying people is to equate them with things—handmade centers or the cheap song embedded in the groove."

A blackbird shadow came across my face. There was the sudden heavy sigh of snow when the tree by the hedge moved in the wind, a white soft dollop of a melted sigh that shifted along the branch, fell to the earth, and vanished in the concealing softness.

Now it is night, deep blue with butterscotch light under the clear folded sky, and the giants are trampling the snow, walking with two or three swift paces across the earth, for it is night, and fairy tales have come to rest, and now I will sleep. Is it the fault of my coal-black pine-forest eyes that I dream of white squirrels brushing their tails over me, or is it only the wind blowing down the reinforcements of snowflakes, the new armies that will keep control of the earth and conceal the truth forever?

3.

"Children are ripe for smiling. Those living in the Council Flats around the corner have sallow faces and streaky hair and their clothes have chopped hems, but they go hand in hand, Snowman, hitting each other and grasping and hugging and then suddenly running away. You will not know how it feels to be a child walking with your elder sister and to have your elder sister suddenly begin to run and run until she disappears around the corner leaving you alone in the street with the buildings so tall beside you and fierce dogs with black noses parading up and down, and cars and lorries growling by, and stern-looking women in purple hats and blue aprons, out sweeping their share of pavement, and telling you to mind, mind, and what else are you doing but minding? People learn the technique of vanishing when they are so young. They rock into and out of sight and when they are gone, when you cannot see them, then perhaps they are dead or drowned in the rain barrel. Vanishing is always magic. Now you see me, now you don't, people say, laughing, and their laughter is cruel.

"Has my sister gone away forever? the little girl thinks. Or is she just around the corner, up the street where I cannot see her?

"How can she tell?

"People vanish and never return, people vanish and return, but each vanishing brings unhappiness. And then when people finally vanish, when they are dead, they are brought determinedly within sight, captured, enclosed, while everyone persists in saying that they are gone and will never return. It is very confusing and contradictory, Snowman."

Another morning. My overcoat changed, clean and white, the snow blinked from my eyes. I am pleased that the technique of vanishing does not concern me. I am so permanently established here that I would not believe vanishing was possible if I did not observe it happening each day—

around corners, into the sky, behind doors, gates, hedges; the smiles, greetings, alarm, anger, vanish from faces; even the visiting wind wearing his cloak of snow, a generous gift from the night sky, has played vanishing tricks with yesterday's carpet and all the footprints, ridges, patterns impressed upon it. The morning earth is freshly decked from floor to ceiling with new white upholstery, white cushions, covers, wall hangings, the earth is a vast white room with the wind and his brothers lounging in every deep chair, drinking snow-tasting tea out of the gray and white china clouds. It is very civilized and ceremonious, I am sure.

"Just think. In a few days it will have vanished, we'll never know it was there."

That is a passer-by speaking. What does he mean? Who are people to make such menacing remarks about snow?

"That man lives across the road with his wife, his daughter, his mother-in-law and her husband. People live in clusters like poisonous berries. The mother-in-law is the head of the house because she wears a purple hat and a blue apron and sweeps their share of the pavement and carefully closes the gate when the postman and the milkman have left it open. She makes strangled cries to children in danger in the street. Her face is almost overshadowed now by the thrusting bone-shape which will command it when it is a mean-nosed skeleton with dark worked-out mines for eyes. It is strange to think that she resembles most of the other middle-aged women in the street, yet they are not related, but all possess domineering bones impatient to be rid of the tired webbing flesh with its yellow-ochre tint which appeared gradually as the cloudy colors of time were poured into the smooth golden morning mixture; people do not stay young, milky, and dandelion.

"Mrs. Wilbur belongs to the Church and for Jumble Sales, Special Evenings, Harvest and Christmas Festivals, she displays a poster inside her front window, ALL ARE WELCOME. She goes to church for the company of God and of people, for the socials and meetings and 'drives.' In the evening she watches television with her husband, and during the day she has her shopping and cleaning and polishing, and her granddaughter Linda to look after while her mother, Dorothy, goes into town. Yet I don't think I answer your question, Snowman. Who are these people? Their being is more elusive than separate handmade centers or the top of the pop song swatted like a fly into the record. The young couple have a son who boards at a special school and is home during the holidays. He is Mark, that is, a stain or blot or saint. He is always afraid that his mother will vanish, and he screams for long periods in the day and the night, and when she takes him to the shops his cry is Carry me, Carry me, but Dorothy is sharp and stern for the people at the special school have told her to treat Mark as if he were an ordinary child of seven, not to give him cause to believe that he is different, not to 'give in' to him—giving in is a kind of balloon collapse where people see their power escaping from them into the air and being seized by others who have no right to it—but to accept him 'as he is,' to be calm, casual, unobtrusively loving.

" 'I can't carry you. You're seven! I mean, you can walk, Mark love, it's only to the shops and back.'

" 'Carry me, carry me!'

" 'Don't be silly. Take my hand.'

" 'Carry me, carry me, carry me!'

"At the sound of the little boy's cries people living near open their windows and front doors and look out.

" 'It's Mark Wilbur.'

"They say his name aloud, pleased with the certainty of it, for if he is Mark Wilbur then he can't be any of their own children, can he, the ones who go cheerfully to school each morning, who can speak intelligibly, who play with other children and stand up for their share of everything, who will perhaps (like Rosemary) pass their eleven-plus and go to grammar school.

" 'It's Mark Wilbur. Home for the holidays. The little girl is rather sweet isn't she?'

"That is Linda, four. One numbers people for so long then one ceases to number them, but when people die they are always given their correct numbers. Ron Smith, forty-four, suffered a heart attack. Peter Lyon, seventeen, was in collision with a van driven by Herbert Kelly, fifty-five. It is a kind of code, a time-attention and bribery. Linda has fluffy brown hair. She wears billowy clothes and velvet hair ribbons. She is allowed to help grandma put out the empty milk bottles in the morning although she cannot quite reach the window sill where grandma places them, beyond the contamination of the street. Linda is so good. She behaves. When Mark is home he smashes the milk bottles, deliberately. Actions which are carried out deliberately are so hard to forgive, even by a mother who knows her child is different. And grandma busy dusting or sweeping in her purple hat and blue apron, does not always understand.

"'I was looking out the window, Dorothy, dusting the sill, and I saw him snatch the milk bottle from Linda and smash it. He did it deliberately.' Dorothy is silent. There is no defense for deliberate misbehavior, therefore she slaps Mark across the ears or the face while Linda watches smiling, feeling so good and well-mannered in her billowy dress and velvet hair ribbon. Mark begins to scream. He will not stop screaming. His mother drags him inside. The people close their front doors and windows.

"'She'll be glad when he goes back to that special school.'

"'Carry me, carry me!'

"You must admit, Snowman, that there is something to be said for riding in a chariot, and who can blame the child for insisting upon what is perhaps the first right of his life? Yet now he must wait so many years before anyone will again carry him, and then what a solemn expensive duty it will be! I think that if I were human I should want to be carried, like Mark Wilbur. Every morning Mark's father climbs into his vermilion car that is balanced like a clot of blood upon the snow, and he addresses the car, 'Carry me, carry me,' and no one punishes him or tells him not to be ridiculous, that he is old enough to carry himself.

"And when people are asleep they cry 'Carry me, carry me' to their dreams and their dreams carry them and no one complains, for dreams are secret. Yet for the real pomp and pleasure, the final satisfaction of their lifelong desire, people must wait until they are dead.

"Carry me. It is the prerogative of the dead, Snowman.

You know, don't you, what has happened in the house two doors away on this side of the street? Are you too busy being flattered by the children who lick your hand to see what you taste like and find you taste like soot—how can snow taste like soot?"

"I am no more than a snowman. People are not my concern, I do not even know my creator. All I know is that she is thirteen, goes to Grammar School, and fell in love with a University student who wore a long striped scarf. Her father is a telephonist who cannot get through to Paris, Rome, Marseilles. Her mother has a blouse shop, subscribes to the *Amateur Gardener* and the annual *Flower Arrangement Calendar* and has two geraniums growing in pots outside the back door."

"If you know as much as that, Snowman, then you easily complete the picture, play the human game with the human focus. I wanted to tell you that Sarah Inchman is dead; she died one night and you never knew because you are not yet able to read the signs or join the dots."

"Why should I? I am only a snowman. I shall live for ever. I do not care if Sarah Inchman is dead. What were the signs which my coal-black pine-forest eyes refused to interpret?"

"The other day the doctor made two visits to the house, the second visit outside his normal hours, and when he was leaving Thomas Inchman came to the door with him and walked bareheaded through the snow to the car. You ask what is strange about that? When Thomas Inchman stands bareheaded and without an overcoat or gloves far from his front door and in the freezing air with snow on the ground and threats of snow in the sky, then it is a sign that he is in distress. He seemed more helpless perhaps because he is going bald and the blue light cast upon his head from the sky and the snow seemed to draw the blue veins nearer his scalp so that his head seemed fragile and in great danger like a baby's head with the fontanel not closed and no one to protect it. He stood there beyond the time it would usually take for him to say, 'Thank you, Doctor,' and for the doctor to answer, 'Right. Call me if there's a change for the worse.' While Thomas Inchman seemed helpless in the blue light the doctor seemed self-possessed; he wore a heavy tweed overcoat and a warm brown hat made of furry material and his gloves were fur-lined and his Indian skin showed warm and brown and alive and his hands held the rich brown leather briefcase in a secure grip. He drew up the collar of his overcoat as if enticing the forces of life closer to him, and he smiled sympathetically at Thomas Inchman, yet at the same time there was a flash of triumph in his glance. He climbed into his car, started the engine, and was away with the powerful car moving effortlessly through the snowy street where only the same morning other cars had been abandoned.

"When the doctor had visited for the third time and Thomas had once again watched him drive away, he returned to the house and drew the curtains in the ground-floor-front room, not closing them casually with gaps of light shining between them but sealing them as if they were made of an impenetrable metal which only a desperate strength would cleave in order to admit the murky snow-filled daylight.

"People passing in the street may not have realized that Sarah Inchman was dead, but if they had stopped to take notice they would have sensed the disorganization of the household. Robert's car stood outside. Robert is the son. Robert came home only at weekends. Why was he home now, in daylight when people who should be at work were at work and the only movement of traffic was of heavy lorries trying to get through to Peckham, of salesmen passing with their cars stacked with samples, rag-and-bone men on their rounds, men from the Water Board making their strange probing inspections through the snowfall. All these were legitimate travelers but not sons arriving home in broad daylight when their usual practice was to come on Friday evening after dark.

"If you did not guess, Snowman, by seeing Robert's car, you would surely have known if you had seen Robert, for the wind was bitterly cold, the flakes were falling, and Robert was clad in a heavy overcoat, and why should he not be? When the doctor drew his overcoat closer to his body he was confidently enticing the forces of life; when Robert turned up the collar of *his* coat he seemed to be trying to repel the forces of death, his coat seemed to be worn with no thought for outward weather, and his reliance upon it was not born of his need to escape from the snow. With the collar turned up, all the buttons buttoned, the lapels drawn close together, he had a total appearance of helplessness. The coat was black-and-white-checked tweed. Woven with snowflakes? The enemy had penetrated the weave and lay snug on Robert's back.

"Yesterday Thomas Inchman kept coming to the front

door of his home, walking out, still not dressed for the weather, and peering up and down the street as if he were waiting for someone. His son came and went, came and went, shuttling his car back and forth from here to there with the restlessness brought on by grief. If you had observed all these incidents, and the house with the feverish hanging light shaped like a crystal ball burning behind the impenetrable curtains, and if you had not divined the nearness of death, surely you would have known when darkness fell (like an ax) and a sprightly little black van drew up outside the Inchman house. The writing on the side of the van was almost concealed in the gloom of night.

"Funeral Service and Furnishings.

"In this part of the world, Snowman, dying is meant to be a discreet matter like taking tea but the untidiness of death makes itself visible in the clothes of the bereaved, in the daily routine—yesterday's milk not opened or even collected, the television silent, the beds unmade. In spite of people's desire for death to be a neat occasion—what is neater than dying?—there are always slovenly obtrusions which mar the effect.

"The funeral will be held tomorrow. Everything will be in order. The undertaker in the sprightly black van will have arranged everything. All is quiet now in the Inchman house. There was a time that when members of a family died they were abandoned, and their relatives packed their bundles and fled over the plain or desert to reach the friendly oasis by nightfall, and there, seeming to forget the dead, the little group would make their meal and then huddle together looking up at the stars that were wild beasts—lions, bears, wolves—prowling the shifting cloud-fields where even the white grass and trees never stay and the cities of fire are trampled by the restless sparking hoofs. And the family would fall asleep and in the morning they did not weep for the dead for the dead had no share in the living but were alone, already becoming a part of the plain or the desert with the shadows of the wings of the vultures wheeling over the earth like great broad blades of a wind-mill set in motion by winds blowing from beyond the frontiers of death to draw new forces of life from the mingled grass and sand and dead human flesh.

"The dead are not abandoned here, Snowman. It is not the fashion to abandon them until it is certain that they are decently covered and imprisoned. Yet the urge to escape from them is always overwhelming. Sarah Inchman has been taken to the chapel mortuary. Thomas and Robert have gone to stay with Sarah's niece and her family in Lewisham. If you looked carefully inside the house you would notice the telltale marks of flight, of haste, which would differ only in surface detail from the traces left by the bereaved tribe in the desert or the plain; you would sense the same underlying urgency to escape from the presence and the place of the dead."

"But I am only a snowman. Death is no concern of mine, but the world grows more depressing each day that I live. Why should I who am destined to live forever be troubled by this finality which touches every human being? I am only a snowman with a head and belly full of snow. I have no means of wandering in plains and deserts or in the rooms of houses where the dead have lain. I am pleasurably heavy and sleepy, I will forget death, I am in a blue daze, tasted by rosy children, my limbs amputated and replaced by mischievous schoolboys. Soon I shall be photographed. Life is soft white bliss and the snow is falling away from my face with my laughter."

4.

"It is night. Here in the city the light has blue shadows under its eyes and stays up late and wanders restlessly from street to street picking up the shadows standing lonely on corners and in alleyways. The eyes of city light are bloodshot with watching. People depend so much upon the light to reveal to them the shadows and the dust which they have been careless in not sweeping away or laying shrouds against, and other people's faces which demand the most brilliant searchlight beams in order that their identity may be established. When you are walking in the street it is so important to know who passes close to you. When you are sitting at night in the same room or sleeping in bed side by side it is important to be able to recognize your companion. There are many strangers about, Snowman. Who knows? And there is also death by accident or intention in the dark. In the streets of the city they have built arcs of light which shine like gorse bushes in bloom, seen through the red haze of a bush fire; the street lights burst upon the street beneath them in thorns and blooms and twigs of red-and-gold light that stabs and changes—like a drug administered—the aspect of all color. Tonight, Snowman, you are not snow, you are sunset; sunset and dragons."

"It is the first time you have mentioned the sun."

"Your nature as a snowman will reveal the sun to you soon enough. Let us talk of the night and the dragon-light which shines on you. Yet it is no use, Snowman, when events happen they appropriate the time to themselves, stealing days, months, years when a few minutes would be enough to satisfy them but there is no stopping them—what are we to do?"

"I need do nothing. I am only a snowman. It is people who are in danger."

"One might say that a person takes a few seconds to die, and there can be no objection if someone wishes to claim a few seconds from the store of time, one might almost say it is a reward for dying, to sleep at last with a few seconds gathered like a posy of flowers upon one's breast, but the notion is false and people realize it, for it is death which takes the few seconds, and once death takes a handful of time there is no amount of minutes, days, years which will satisfy his greed; in the end he takes a lifetime. I wanted to talk to you about the night and the street lights, but I notice that the death of Sarah Inchman is at large prowling for more time, turning our attention to the Inchman house as surely as the wind turns the weather vane. Robert has come home tonight. He is aware of the prowling death of his mother, therefore he has secured the windows and fastened the chains across the front and back doors. He is sitting by the fire trying to read his book of science fiction but he is thinking about his mother and her clothes. What will he do about her clothes?

"Dr. Merriman held up the globe of the world in all its

blues browns greens reds and spun it lightly with his fingers. He withdrew his hand. The world continued spinning, faster and faster. Dr. Merriman smiled. My God, he thought. He knew and the others in the room knew. The holtrime, the wentwail, the sturgescene had . . .

"Why were her clothes such a drab color? The clothes of the one or two women he had brought home had been as bright as bird-of-paradise plumage, and his mother's clothes too had seemed gay. Where were all the blues and greens and pinks that she wore in the weekend when he came home? Why could he not find the bright clothes she had worn? Had he dreamed them? If that was so then was he also enchanted in looking at the rest of the world?

> The fenew is cardled. The blutheon millow
> clane or hoven. In all the dolis gurnt plange
> dernrhiken ristovely; Kentage, merl,
> the fenew is cardled, onderl,
> pler with dallow,
> dimt, in amly wurl.

"Why was it that as soon as his mother died her clothes seemed drab, brittle, that burnt brown color like beetle shells found in the grass in September?

"Like a collapsed armor?

"The fenew is cardled. Dr. Merriman twirled the hollow globe faster and faster.

"That is science fiction, Snowman. Soon there will be a visitor from outer space."

"But I am such a visitor or am I old-fashioned?"

"No, Snowman, you are just as modern as the little green

man with black horns. But now that the death of Sarah Inchman has ceased her prowling and has entered her son's thoughts for the profit to be had from his dreams, we can talk once again of the night and the street lights, but most of the people in the street are asleep now, and the lights in the houses have gone out and there is no more gunfire from the television sets. The fresh evening fall of snow, like a cat set before a saucer of milk, has lapped up all the wheel and foot marks and the street has a sunken smooth appearance and with few cars and people braving the snowfall only the wind and the wandering animals and the deaths in search of extra time have the pleasure of making patterns on the snow, while you, Snowman, are growing plumper and plumper and your brass buttons are covered with new snow and your coal-black pine-forest eyes are hooded with snowy brows.

"What a drifting careless life of snowflakes flying heedlessly without effort or decision. And I am remembering as a snowflake myself the time when I too was a visitor from beyond the earth. I remember how some of my companions alighted upon a cold stone doorstep and they seemed to vanish into it, while others died before they arrived on earth. There was a movement of their bodies, a sparkle through the white shadow of their secret crystal skeleton, a sudden falling away of their flesh, now a sweetness, now a trace of salt in the air as the released bones crinkled, snapped starlike, disappeared. I remember—but Memory like Death has a way of seizing time. Do not be alarmed, Snowman, if soon the snow changes color. Now it lies with breathing space for each flake, but within the next few days the flakes may be churned together, one may smother its neighbor while a gray or black liquid oozes from their bodies, and people will say it is the snow bleeding in its true color, black blood.

"I am warning you what to expect, for this evening I feel the touch of a wind that is an enemy of snow, that does not breathe the penetrating freezing breath which is the delight of snowflakes. Tonight there is a warm wind blowing from the south from the world where the olive trees grow, their gray shadows falling like flakes upon the gray stone, where the red earth crumbles like the hot ashes of a fire, and yellow flowers bloom in the dried river beds; where the eucalyptus trees lean above the stone fountain and the soft dust stirs about the feet of the people walking; a world of salt marshes, hills of salt, beanflowers, almond blossom, tiny pine trees with sticky purple flowers and small syrup-oozing cones; spotted poisonous toadstools that collapse when you touch them, clouding your face with a yellow mist, toadstools with tall extravagant stems the result of spurted growth which makes people afraid for they cannot accept the outrage of such furious vegetable growth, believing it should happen only in fairy tales. And when their own children growing up, change and develop as if overnight, people utter such cries of panic, 'He's growing too fast, he'll outgrow his strength, it's not healthy, it's dangerous!'

"I feel the warm wind, Snowman, although it has not yet reached us here in the street of the city. It is fresh from blowing beneath blue skies above blue seas filled with shadowy houses and people and trees and fishing boats that, like people, make their coughing sounds at morning, cough-chug, cough-chug. There is herb-smell in the wind, and the sound of new green frogs, the population explosion of ponds.

"And the sad-looking cow with the rubbed scabbed shoulders and the too-small tethering-rope, has calved and swings and rocks her udder like a bagful of sea.

"It is all in the warm wind blowing from the south. Even if you pleaded with me, Snowman, I should not be able to delay its arrival here. People plant trees against the wind yet it always sneaks in twos and threes of breath through the gaps in the branches and between and beneath the leaves. People have found no way to refuse the wind's gift of blowing; they have discovered only how to establish its direction and force and how to adjust their lives, like sails, to let the wind carry them to the place they most desire to reach before dark. Oh Snowman I have desired to reach so many places! As a Perpetual Snowflake I am powerless and diminished. You never saw me in the height of my life when a thousand snowflakes leaned upon me and found shelter near me. How quiet it is now, you can hear only the city murmur that is not the sound of people but a murmuring like the sea washing the land.

"People live on earth, and animals and birds; and fish live in the sea but we do not defeat the sea for we are driven back to the sky or we stay.

"It is a question of reptiles hatching deep in the warm sand; of flayed shredded brown weed; crushed spiral houses and tall blue-bearded shells; and an old mapped tortoise in the Galapagos Islands that woke one morning to find himself famous. The embezzlements of living—that is the sound of the sea and of the city . . ."

"White flying squirrels brushing my face . . ."

"You are dreaming, Snowman."

5.

"I have learned to recognize the people in the street. I know the milkman, and the meter reader, and the window cleaner, and the postman who is limping with his sore foot. 'I'll have to go on the National Health,' he said, 'or visit the Board.' What does he mean?"

"The Board is not part of a forest but is a room with rows of seats facing a counter which has been divided into cubicles the average height of a person sitting. If you wish to claim a grant from the Board you go to one of these cubicles and answer questions about your income, property, age, occupation, and so on. You will understand, Snowman, that the cubicles have been constructed to ensure privacy, and it seems to have been calculated that personal secrets do not rise above the head of those who possess them, not like warm air which travels to the ceiling or like smell which penetrates the air and the walls and furniture and clothing; it has been assumed that personal secrets have a discretion of their own, that they will roam within the cubicle but never dream of escaping. Nevertheless the people who are being interviewed have not so much trust in their own secrets, for they whisper the details, glancing around them for fear something has escaped.

"'Speak up please, no one can hear you. You're in a cubicle to ensure privacy.'

"The whispering continues.

"That is the Board, Snowman. It can be of little interest to you for it is no relation to a pine forest and it is not more ancient than coal, it is a way of getting money when you have no work, and incidentally of stabling and training secrets so that they do not rise above a man's head.

"Now here is the rag-and-bone man, the totter, sitting in his chair-sized cart surrounded by old striped mattresses stained with rust and blood, by twisted bed ends, fireplaces wrenched at last from their cavern in the wall to make room for the gas or electric heater, blackened fenders, iron bars, bundles of rags. The totter's piebald horse jerks to a stop, the driver rings his brass bell like a priest summoning the communion of refuse; then he cries out but you cannot understand what he has said for surely the purpose of his cry is to distort its meaning and arouse fear in those who are listening. 'What is he saying?' they wonder. 'Is it Bring Out Your Dead? Any old Rags? Old Rags, Old-Ways, Old-Ways, Gold Rags Rays Racks God-racks All Ways? And why does he never mention the bones?'

"There is his brother walking up and down the street to collect the refuse in his sack. The two look like twins and the small lithe horse with its coat of gray and white seems like a third member of the family. One might imagine that the three are interchangeable and that from time to time the brothers take their turns between the shafts of the cart.

"Now they have disappeared around the corner. When it

snows people do not put out their old clothes and bed-
steads and extracted fireplaces with the roots of the wall
still clinging to them. People in snowstorms have other matters to think of; snow fills people's minds and the world,
there is no room for nameless iron bars or mattresses stained
with the residue of sleep and love when the concern is the
residue of sky. Look at the earth now with its fat layers of
wadding, the padded gates and fences with not an iron bone
protruding, and the heavy-headed roofs that will soon discard their weight of snow when the fitted gray slates of
their skulls begin to shift and slide. The pipes are frozen
in the houses. The water has stopped in its tracks. I fear
that the black blood is beginning to flow. Look, there's
a blackbird sitting on an iced twig, singing!"

"I am afraid, though I am only a snowman."

I slept and woke. I tried to think of the pleasures of being
a snowman, to anticipate the delight of being photographed,
but I could not ignore the small trickle of black blood
flowing through the hedge into the gutter. People passing
noticed it and remarked upon it, pointing to it and speaking in tones of excitement and dismay which left me unable
to tell whether they were announcing disaster or victory.
I was standing staring with my coal-black pine-forest eyes
when I saw a woman walking from house to house with a
basket of flowers and I shuddered and bowed my head for
I knew they were daffodils.

"Look, Snowman, at the children crowding around her,
screaming with pleasure, even the little Italian children
from next door who cannot yet speak the language of this

country although Salvatore can say Hello, Good-by, and Milk. 'Milk mama, milk.' He can say bread too which was once yellow in a field, like daffodils, but you need not be too afraid, Snowman, for perhaps they are not real daffodils; it will be many weeks before daffodils can calculate the arrival of their moment and take their place in the dance. Snowdrops are in bud, but snowdrops are made of snow."

"Why does everyone seem so pleased at the sight of the daffodils? Listen!"

"Lovely daffodils, early daffodils, bring yourself good luck and buy a bunch of lovely daffodils from a Gypsy."

"Some will buy the flowers because they rely on their personal sense of time and will not wait until it agrees with the season, and it is those people who can experience spring in winter which may be agreeable, I do not know, yet it is the same people who will dread seeing others surrounded by daffodils with crowns of violets in their hair, while their own hearts are heavy with snow and their eyes cannot keep from gazing at the never-ending shroud wrapped about the world and the dark tomb waiting to admit the dead. All who believe in daffodils while snow falls around them are living uneasily beating lives, their rhythm is the lost note which cannot or will not join the chord because although it will gain security and strength by being with other notes it will at the same time forget the sound of itself, and therefore it stays alone in strange hollow places where there is no other music. The loneliness is the price and the reward."

"Who are the gypsies to sell early daffodils, real or artificial, when there is snow on the ground, when snowmen are in charge of the earth?"

"The gypsies are all people who are out of step with usual time and place, and it is they who are a nuisance, an uneasiness to those who set their hearts by the clock, who stay and divide each day by twenty-four hours and get no surprising untidy scrawl of blossom in the remainder column; for primroses push their way through rusting iron, and new grass is a carpenter's tool, hammer, chisel, axhead, and snowdrops are the first white steel pylons erected to carry the message.

"Gypsies come and go and baffle like the delinquent swarm of bees that does not keep to the seasonal rhyme or rhythm but follows its own signals and smokes itself out of the secret hollow trees."

Although the gypsy seemed in the distance to be an old woman, when she came nearer I saw that she was young. I am learning to guess ages in people, and lately I have longed for a sign that time is noticing me, and each night I have considered every inch of my body, saying to myself, "Has time been here, here—how shall I know?" I stared at a baby in its pram yesterday. Then I looked away at the sky or the street or the shifting ledge of snow on the branch of the tree, and when I looked again at the baby I saw that its red fur cap now framed the face of its mother, and beyond that face like a shadow which is given a shape in darkness by a vivid beam of light shining upon it, was the face of the mother's mother, and then her mother before that, and if I had stared long enough I should have seen the dark space where the first signs of life were imprinted. I am envious of people and their association with time, of the way they can look into each other's eyes and see backward to the first empty darkness or forward to the final sun-blistered collage of light. How does a mere snowman recognize the effect of time upon himself?

The gypsy passed close to me and looked at me.

"When snow falls," she said, "there is always a snowman."

A daffodil dropped from her basket and she did not see it fall, and I thought, that is strange, it is only when people are walking to hell that they can afford to drop flowers in their path. A child picked up the daffodil and stuck it in my hat. I slept with a daffodil in my hat—how brave of me! I could not smell it and it was stiff and shiny and it hurt where the stem thrust into my head. Rosemary was on her way home from school.

"Oh, a daffodil in the snowman's hat!"

She ran to me, withdrew the daffodil, and sniffed it.

"Plastic," she said. "They're everywhere."

I looked about me to see if she spoke the truth but I could see no others in the street or in the sky. When the daffodils come will they be everywhere?

The woman next door looked over the fence.

"Plastic," she echoed. "But they're useful for wall vases or the back of the car. They melt, though, if you put them near the fire."

I remembered vividly the snowman with a fire burning in his head, and the way he sank into the earth and disappeared. Was that death? Had Sarah Inchman died because she leaned too close to a fire?

"What are the signs of death?"

"The signs of death are without nobility or dignity or beauty, they are as shameful as the assenting chalk marks on the rust-red sides of a loaded cattle-truck after men have learned that a cattle-truck will hold more people than cattle, that it will accommodate the whole human race in its journey to the desert over drains and dust and broken stones and dandelions where the milk is sucked by little black flies, while babies with their bones pushing like soft white mushrooms through their flesh, and grown men and women with their bones rising like sharpened axes know nothing of the thin blue trickle of milk flowing through the stem of the dandelion."

"Dandelion milk, mushrooms?"

"People must share the world and the streams which flow through it but if the dead have lain in the streams then to drink from them is death.

"Look at the icicle, Snowman, look above your head at the melting icicle!"

I saw the glistening silver rod wedged between the snow-covered slates of the roof and the spouting slowly begin to move, with its spine breaking, to shudder and writhe while its sharp point which as a weapon might have plunged and driven through my heart, began to disappear and drops of water fell upon the path to mingle with the stream of black blood which was growing wider and swifter and now was surging out into the street, so that even the curious frightened people staring at it were forced to acknowledge the fact of the wound.

Harry Dincer came to his front door. He held a shovel which he thrust before him as if he were angry. I imagined that he had come to help me win some obscure battle, that because his daughter Rosemary had created me, he felt obliged to protect me. His face was flushed, his eyes were streaked with red; he had been down at the King's Arms again drinking away his despair at never being able to say 'Ullo Rome, Paris, Marseilles. He plunged the shovel into the snow and began to clear great masses of snow not caring how he mishandled or crushed it, lurching it forward along the path and into the street to the gutter where it was heaped in a gray sweating mound, like a new grave.

"But you have never seen a grave, Snowman. Sarah Inchman's grave is new, in a Garden of Rest where plastic flowers in shaded alcoves await the fire. The funeral was conducted by tall men in tall black hats and the wreaths were arranged high on the roof of the polished black car —all as a pretense of being able to see into the sky, the conjurer's approach, Snowman, to the magic moment when the jaw drops and the accusing eyes are quickly pressed shut in case they spy and tell. Children sometimes joke to a tall man, 'Is it cold up there?' You, Snowman, who came from the sky, you know how often during the festivals of death you must have seen the polished black chimney pots parading among the clouds and the brittle stars to get a peep at the other world."

When Harry Dincer finished the attack with his shovel he came over to me and I thought for a moment that he would demolish me also. I had no way of defending myself.

"Our snowman," he said. "I forgot about you. It won't

be long now will it? We'll take your photo as soon as we can, while we have the chance."

He looked at the sky.

"More snow today," he said wisely.

"Hi Harry!"

That was the man next door who also works in the telephone exchange but who is allowed on the Continental Circuit and can get through to Rome, Paris, Marseilles almost any time he cares to.

"Hi Max. Never known it to last so long have you?"

"Looks like more tonight, what's up with the weather? Last winter was mild as mild. You been working hard?"

Harry was silent for a few minutes. 'Ullo Rome Paris Marseilles.

"Couldn't sleep," he said. "Racket next door. Thought I'd clear my share of snow."

"I wonder what the Council think they're doing, drifts everywhere."

"How's the job Max?" Harry tried not to show his envy. "Still on the Continental Circuit?"

"Sure."

Harry's eyes filled with longing. Anyone could have told what he was thinking: What really happened when you put on the headphones and began to talk in a different language? To people so far away? And why did they keep showing that advertisement in the newspapers, 'Ullo Rome, Paris, Marseilles, men up to fifty-nine with or without experience. Why fifty-nine? What happened when you were sixty that gave you no hope of ever getting through to Rome, Paris, Marseilles? Max was fifteen years younger than Harry—thirty-seven—and the bald patch on the back of his head was so carefully darned with crisscross strands of hair that you didn't notice it unless you took special care to see it.

"You are learning, Snowman."

Harry made a sudden wrench with his shovel, but I need not have been afraid for he did not attack me.

"See you Max," he called, and went inside.

It snowed and I slept.

6.

"There is talk of simplicity. Snow has made the world simple as deceit is simple, a soft mask concealing the intention and truth of hills and plains and cities, the toil and thrust and rock and stone and grass growing like green ribs to accommodate the sky's breath. A dust-sheet on the restless furniture of the world. You ought to be proud, Snowman, to have so changed the face of the earth, to have reduced it to such a terrible simplicity that people are blinded if they gaze upon it."

Another morning. I am used to morning, to watching the light stealing red-rimmed through the smoke above the chimneys and the white walls of the buildings. I am used to children snatching my arms and my buttons or pipe and replacing them; to the sinister remarks made by people who stop to stare at me. I am used to the comings and goings of the Dincer family. I wonder if Rosemary has forgotten her grieving over the University student.

"Oh, that disappointment about her age?"

"Disappointment! But you said it was the end, you said it was a kind of death!"

"Language wanes, Snowman. Feelings wane. Death comes to be no more than a disappointment, and grief over events must be strictly rationed and the size of the ration is controlled by distance in time and space—the attentions of the heart are measured by the pacing of the feet and the movements of the hands of the clock. The massacre of a race of people is only on the level of a disappointment if it is beyond the range of the stay-at-home feet controlled by the stay-at-home heart beating in time with the familiar clock. When a man puts a telescope to his snow-blinded eye he can see streams of oil flowing and fields of wheat trampled by cloud-shadows driven by the wind, but he can't see the tiny distant ration of his own Care. But no, wait, what is that fluttering speck in his snow-blinded eye? It is a fly, disappointment and death, Care and Love crawling close to his own skin, the source of their lifeblood. Why should they travel to face the flood and the earthquake, the dark camp where the children's bones push soft as mushrooms through their flesh, and the men and women sharpen their gaunt axes upon the human stone?"

"Now Rosemary is walking sedately home from school. Her manner of walking comes easily to her for she has practiced it during the years she was at Primary School, and now when she walks as a Grammar School girl she is preparing for the time when she will be a University student. As she walks she flings her long striped University scarf over her shoulder. Don't believe that people live in the present, Snowman. There is haste for tomorrow and the need to know how to behave when tomorrow comes. Walking like a University student is simple; and dressing like one; and later living and behaving like a wife, a mother, a career woman; knowing the clothes to wear, the smile to adopt, the opinions to discuss and agree or disagree with, the people to make happy or unhappy from the limited ration of Love and Care. But what is the correct behavior for Death? Whom will Rosemary imitate in order to die? There is no clue for her except in her own sleep and dreams, for one imitates one's own death, and when the time comes Rosemary cannot borrow her grandmother's way of dying or her grandfather's or her Uncle Phil's or Sarah Inchman's.

"Now Rosemary is outside the gate. She sees Doris, a girl of her own age, walking on the opposite side of the road. As they go to different Grammar Schools and are not yet used to the strangeness, they like to spend their after-school hours, weekends, and holidays working delicate but swiftly fading patterns into their former Primary School friendship by embroidering their anxieties and new experiences. Now they call out and wave and smile to each other, and forgetting her Grammar School dignity Rosemary runs to talk to Doris. Her feet crunch upon the hardened snow. She slips and falls in an ice-filled trough of snow. The heavy lorry has no time to swerve or stop.

"And that, Snowman, is death.

"See how there is no concentration, no tension, only diffuseness, untidiness. There is no rigid drop of death congealed upon the surface of living, no stain that one may point to and try to erase. It is this elusiveness of death, the vacuum created when it happens that cause details, incidents, emotions of living people to flood in filling the emptiness and crowding the untidiness with a further disarray. From up and down the street, from beyond, around corners, out of front and back doors people come running toward the scene all with their contribution of irrelevance. One woman has a tea towel in her hand, another a shopping bag, the man over the road is still holding his half-sewn overcoat, the school children carry their cases and satchels. In a way they seem like refugees from the vague unimportant outer circle trying to reach a clarity and significance at the dark still center. But where is the center, the perfect stain of the moment? They cannot find it. Curtains are drawn aside. Those who have not chosen to join the crowd are staring from their windows, and one has telephoned 999 which is easier to contact than Paris, Rome, or Marseilles. Police ambulance fire. The lorry driver is sitting in the snow, quietly and sadly, as if his home were the snow and the snow were his doorstep where he sits in the evening looking out upon the world. The spectators seem to realize the driver's right to that small area of snow, for they avoid it and make detours about it. But the walls of the lorry driver's white house are made of glass and he can see out and the people can see in and their eyes are full of pity. They say, 'What will we do, What will we do?'

"One man from the crowd is standing on guard beside Rosemary. He has felt for her pulse. He has placed his hand on her forehead, not because it will help or explain her condition but because his mother used to touch his own

forehead when he was a child and felt sick. Everyone is
staring at him, trying to read the expression on his face.
"Listen, Snowman."

Like a dog yelping, I thought it was a dog and then I saw
the navy coat and her in a heap.
They've rung for the ambulance.
Who rang?
I don't know. Someone, I don't know.
Is the ambulance coming?
I think so, someone rang for it.
Has someone called the ambulance?
Is there someone seeing to everything?
I suppose so, I should think so, definitely so.
I suppose the ambulance is on its way?
More than likely. Someone will have rung for it.
They're waiting for the ambulance. It shouldn't be long.
Did someone ring for it?
I think so, someone rang for it.
Who rang for it?
Someone who saw it happen.
Did you see it?
No, I was just turning the corner when I heard the
screeching noise and a funny thing I was thinking how
slippery the snow was just there. . . .
There?
Yes, just there, and someone screamed.
Look at the lorry driver.
Yes, just sitting there.
He's ill with shock. They've been trying to get him to
move but he won't.

He just stays there.

Her parents are at work aren't they? Her mother runs that little blouse shop down at the Green.

I believe so. Maisy's.

There's someone coming, it looks like an ambulance.

I think it is. Someone rang for it, someone over there.

I suppose it was the man who's standing near her.

Did he ring for the ambulance?

Someone said it was him. They say he says she's dead.

The girl Dincer isn't it?

Yes, she goes to Grammar School, her mother keeps the blouse shop down at the Green.

Daisy's?

No, Maisy's. She owns it with her sister.

Didn't her father sell you that old television that never went?

It was the tubes, and such a lot of interference.

We had a man in two weeks ago, I'm getting tired of it.

Look the lorry driver's getting up. Someone's helping him into that house. I wonder how he'll face her parents?

I can hear a bell ringing. It's the ambulance. It's taken ages.

Someone must have rung for it.

I think someone did.

There's the Dincer car with Mrs. Dincer driving.

And here's the ambulance. Look they're getting out the stretcher. Look, the man's shaking his head.

Isn't it awful with everyone staring, like a circus. They should tell everybody to go away, some people have no respect for privacy.

Look he's shaking his head again.

They're covering up her face. I guessed it. She must be dead.

There's a blanket over her face.

Did they say she was dead?

Someone said. They said that man said who put that coat over her to start with.

Look he's talking to the Dincers. I won't be able to walk past there today or ever.

There's blood on the snow. It's a funny green color. The police make a fuss don't they, they have to.

They're clearing the snow, putting things in order.

All the same I can't walk past there.

Did the Dincers go in the ambulance with her?

I didn't see. More than likely. I wonder who rang for the ambulance?

Someone must have rang.

They've taken the lorry driver to hospital too.

Why have the police put lanterns there, as if it's night?

They always do. It's dark early but in a few weeks the days will be longer, have you decided about this year?

No, we're waiting, though they say book early but there's always room when the time comes.

I wouldn't be too sure though. It's their only daughter too.

She goes to Grammar School.

Did they really say she was dead?

It looks like it. You could tell really though couldn't you? Who was that man in the brown coat who took charge? He doesn't live in the street.

He looks like a foreigner. A total stranger.

He had his wits about him. Did you see it happen?

No, I was just coming around the corner when I heard the scream.

They say she ran over to meet her friend, the girl Miller. Doris Miller. They've taken her away too.

Have they?

Yes, that woman who rang for the ambulance took her inside.

Did that woman ring for the ambulance? I thought it was the man in the corner house. I had the impression it was him.

Him? No, it was that woman. They say she rang for the ambulance. And then she was out there talking to the ambulance men as if she'd rung.

Then she must have. She'd ring 999 I suppose and they'd get through. I suppose that's how the police came.

Are they leaving the lanterns there? It's not dark.

It will be. The snow makes it darker. I've never known it to snow for so long, not in the city, all night and all day and the Council have had to bring in casual labor to deal with it.

Yes, men with beards and tramps. Hear the bell?

Yes, perhaps it's the ambulance on the way to King's.

No, it will have got there ages ago, it must be another ambulance.

Perhaps there's been another accident.

More than likely. They shouldn't have these heavy lorries in the snow.

It was stupid of her to run across of course. She wasn't
exactly a child. She goes to Grammar School.

Her mother has that blouse shop down at the Green.

Maisy's?

No, Daisy's.

The police must have rung for her.

Or the hospital when someone rang for the ambulance.

Who rang for the ambulance?

Wasn't it that man who was standing near her, the one
who took charge. I've never seen him before.

A perfect stranger.

Well someone rang anyway. Her father's a telephonist.
They'd get through to him quick enough.

Yes they'd ring the exchange.

The ambulance people?

No, the police or the woman who rang the ambulance.

Didn't the man ring?

Well someone rang anyway but I don't suppose they
could do anything for her.

I saw the man shaking his head.

They put a blanket over her face, one of those gray
blankets.

They shouldn't have done that in full view. It let us
know she was dead, they shouldn't have let everybody
see she was dead, they should have taken her in the
back of the ambulance as if she were ill or something
and would recover.

I don't suppose they thought at the time.

But it let everybody know she was dead, and it makes
things worse to know. It would have been better to

read about it afterward in the paper, as if she had died in hospital.

But they couldn't keep it from people, they couldn't keep it from the parents, not with them standing there.

It doesn't seem right though. To think she was lying there dead all the time!

I couldn't go past there.

They're measuring. Why are they measuring?

It's to do with the inquiry.

They'll want witnesses.

Yes, they'll ask over the B.B.C. You hear them in the morning before the eight o'clock news.

Well I didn't see it thank goodness.

Neither did I, I was just turning the corner. I heard it though.

Don't.

Whoever rang the ambulance must have seen it for them to ring the ambulance.

Yes, I wonder who rang the ambulance?

I am only a snowman. What must a snowman do? I will sleep; there is news of other seasons.

7.

"I saw a fiercely burning light flying beyond the clouds, and the shadow of it passed across my body, and tears ran down my cheeks. I shivered, and my flesh seemed to drop from me and soak into the snow at my feet, and then I think I fell asleep for two days, and when I woke it was morning.

Just as I was waking a wind shook loose one of my coal-black pine-forest eyes and blew it onto the pavement where a black cat sneaked up to it, pounced at it and sent it flying under the hedge into the deep snow and there it lay until a little dog bounded along, scratched at the snow and finding my coal-black pine-forest eye he put it in his mouth where it was held prisoner until the little dog ran home to his owner and dropped my coal-black pine-forest eye at his feet.

"Coal, good boy," she exclaimed, and taking it into her sitting room she placed it upon an interesting mound of other coal-black pine-forest eyes. You have not explained what happened then, Perpetual Snowflake. I do not find my partial loss of sight very distressing; one coal-black pine-forest eye will serve me as well as two.

"While I was asleep I dreamed I was a snowflake again, a tiny flat Peter-Paul tissue of snow with zigzags of air, like melting lace, binding the edges of my body, and I was tucked up in the sky under a soft blanket of cloud and there was no thought of conquering the earth or the sea and no idea that I would ever be a snowman witnessing the comings and goings of people upon their curiously snow-white earth."

"Yes, you slept, Snowman, for two days. If you were being affected by time you would discover that as you grew older you would spend more of your life sleeping. I believe time is affecting you, Snowman, accumulating like layers of snowstorms upon your life. People long to shut their eyes. They yawn. They shade their faces from the snow. In old age they curl up like leaves and sleep beneath drifts of snow and have no care.

"But I had meant to tell you that you have been photographed, you have had what they call your 'likeness' taken."

"My likeness? Taken?"

"Oh there is only one of you, no part of you has been stolen, although keeping alive is a matter of greed more than of loneliness. There is one of each creature because that creature devours all others, it roams through the world with its magnetic mouth seizing the tiny filed brightnesses which are the commencement of others of its kind. You think that you observe other creatures—you have seen many people in the street, little dogs, birds flying or perched here on your tree (your tree!) with their feet plodged in a smooth spreading of snowflake sauce. But if you observe with your invisible eye you will know that to each creature there is only one—himself. The wind blowing from life and death puffs one being to the size of the world. The sky fits him like a skin, and the surface of the earth is only as wide as the soles of his feet or the grasp of his claws, and his wing-span is east and west, north and south, and his head is forever burned by the neighboring flames of the sun. Strangely enough, Snowman, this proud lonely greed is a condition of love as well as of hate, for the self does not know where to stop, it devours friend and enemy."

"But I am only a snowman. I have been photographed. Has it changed me to have had my likeness taken?"

"A snowman, and afraid of change!

"While you were asleep Rosemary was buried, and yesterday, the day of the funeral, Harry looked out of the window and catching sight of you he exclaimed to his wife, 'We never took a photo of it. We promised to make a photo of it while it lasted. I think we ought to take a snap of it now, Kath. Before the warm weather comes and there is a thaw.'

" 'Yes, the snow's going,' Kath said. 'Be quick, Harry, we don't want to be seen taking photos at a time like this, it will make people wonder.'

" 'If we don't take it now it will never get taken, you know how snowmen vanish, one moment they're in front of you large as life the next moment they've vanished.'

"Harry found his camera, came into the garden, focused, clicked the shutter, and your photograph was taken. I assure you it won't hurt you, Snowman. It's just a flat impression of you, not as important as the shadow which remains by your side here in the garden and which changes its shape according to the light in the sky, now it grows corpulent with morning, now it braves the decapitations of noon and ends a starved evening shape with its fingers clawing at the sky."

As he spoke of the sky I looked up and with my one coal-black pine-forest eye I saw such a dazzle and it was an icicle starred like a frozen wand and I could see a pink and light and deep-blue world enclosed in it, and all the colors of the rainbow were gathered inside, knocking on the glass walls to get free, and then I heard a sharp crack, a sun-groan, and the colors burst suddenly from the icicle and water ran down my face onto my shoulders and down my body to my feet where it changed to black blood.

"What does it mean? Is it a sign because I have been photographed?"

"You need not be afraid of having had your photo taken. The photo failed. It did not come out."

"It did not come out?"

"No, it was misty and blurred, and everything which was not covered with snow appeared white in the photograph while everything white, including yourself, showed as a black shape encircled by a jagged rim of pale light. Solid brick, wood and stone were rendered unsubstantial, became part of a landscape of nothingness, while everything covered with snow—you and your fellow snowflakes who are so sensitive to the prospect of daffodils and fire and sun and warm winds from the south, who are unable to resist even the lightest breath of wind, all that is fragile became strong and bold, as certain as stone and steel, capable of withstanding ordeal by season and sun. That was your photograph, Snowman. It was a failure, it did not 'turn out,' and yet your photo was 'taken' and no one will ever be able to explain the nature of what the camera discovered within you to represent your body as a pillar of black stone in a garden where the branches of a black sword were growing from the earth beneath a sky full of prowling glossy black tomcat clouds; where the solid buildings melted into nothingness, doors, fences, gates, cars, including ambulances, and people dancing or resting or dead, all dissolving before the light-bribing eye of the camera. I hope you are not disturbed when I tell you that your photograph suffered the humiliation of most projects that fail—projects of light, conscience, time, discovery—it was burned quickly on the fire. It flared and crumpled enveloped in a translucent white flame which changed the photo from a cloud of light to a black brittle substance curled at the edges like a stale crust thrown out for the drooling mumbling pigeons—hear them? —that have lost the desire to fly and only potter about in people's heads making white messes in the attics of thought.

"But I wonder, Snowman, I can't tell you precisely what you lost through the burning of your photograph. I have said it is so necessary to be careful in one's observations, to question the actions of people because they do prefer most of all to be comfortable whether in the matter of truth or of toilet. And projects are considered failures because it might take too much time and energy to prove they are successes. Would you rather have an image of yourself as black stone (it might even be marble!) or as white nothingness? I myself am impressed by this bewitching process which extracts stone from snow, swords and knives from trees, and sets the sky wailing with old dark toms padding in and out of the winds that are huddled and tangled, like thorn hedges, about the borders of night."

"How will the point of view of the photograph affect the death of Rosemary? She did not melt or change to snow, at least not when I looked at her with my coal-black pine-forest eyes. Is there a means of photographing death which changes it to life, as objects are changed in the photograph?"

"But the objects were not changed, Snowman. You are still a snowman. It was the view of them—have you ever heard people speak of a view? When they choose where to live they often say, 'It must have a good view.' People like to look at the sea; it flashes and shuffles the silver cards, it winks with enticement, with light, with promise. It deals out peace and speckled flowers pink and blue and rakes in the losses, deep deep, and the losses are secret and no one ever learns the extent of them."

"I know of the sea. People live on earth, and animals and birds, and fish live in the sea but we do not defeat the sea for we are driven back to the sky or we stay and become what we have tried to conquer. . . ."

"That is true, Snowman. The victor has a habit of assuming the identity of those he has vanquished. It is a habit of people also, and animals and birds and bright red fish."

"Do I understand the sea because I have arrived on land? Is that a focus where the true balance of knowing is brought into view?"

"You forget or you do not realize, Snowman, that most photographs 'turn out,' that is, most objects appear as they appear to everyone everywhere. The moment when the picture seems to fail or where the process is arrested before the picture is developed is one of the most exciting moments in the life of a human being. The damp blurred distorted film, the unexpected 'failed' view of the familiar, bring the danger of happiness, and you may know that happiness is a great danger in the lives of people, and that they are prepared from birth to fight and overcome it, to protect themselves from it with shields, hoods, specially fitted secret claws and stings.

"Rosemary is dead. Her death is no real concern of ours because we are made of snow, but if we were flesh and blood we might be tempted to color and retouch her death and place it beside other events instead of giving it a startling isolation upon a blank page.

"No photograph can alter the fact of Rosemary's death but it is likely that the focus of Kath and Harry has been altered. Violent happenings, sudden griefs upset the development of the scene often subjecting it to so much violent overexposure that the result is a view of nothingness. If this happens in the Dincer family, Harry will feel his body falling apart, like straw, or shredded like the weave of sacking. His hair will change to white cotton floating away on the wind and when he clenches his fist the flesh of his hand will melt. He will be a true snowman. The same changes will occur in his wife. Nothing will finally become nothing. And then when all creatures and objects are cleaned of their parasitical identity, why, then the rhymes will have reason. If all the world were paper, if all the seas were ink, if all the trees were bread and cheese—what a marvelous freedom of view that would be, Snowman!

"Kath and Harry may experience a little of this changed world but it is likely that their landscape will emerge in conventional form with death as a recognizable creature, perhaps a member of the family, and with the space in the snow where Rosemary lay after the accident, cleared and new snow scattered there to make it seem as if nothing had happened, as in those photographs which are arranged and retouched with people blotted from the scene if their presence is likely to cause embarrassment to themselves or to others. Memory is quite a useful agent for retouching scenes made complicated or dangerous by grief or happiness, and when people have photographs of others whose eyes reveal too much love or hate it is a convenient trick to make them unrecognizable by concealing their eyes with a strip of tape, as in official photographs of people in prison or in places for the insane. People with too much emotion in their eyes are usually prisoners under sentence and often halfway to losing their reason."

"Snowman, Snowman, the sheet of snow is wearing thin. Were the season a good housewife she would halve the snow and 'turn' it to give the worn places a rest from wear, and she would darn the holes with tiny snow-stitches, and then once again spread the sheet over the earth and the snow would appear brand-new; but the season is not a thrifty housewife; the snow is wearing thin, and there is no one to change top to bottom or inside to outside. Grass is poking through the holes in the material; the flannelette has lost its fleecy lining. The linen is dirty, for the season has slept too long in it. During the next few days if you look high in the sky you will see the first white cleaned clouds being unparceled and set adrift. Are you afraid to look now in the sky? Remember, Snowman, although your photograph did not turn out, they have the negative of you where your appearance is very strange because neither you nor your shadow can be identified unless the negative is held up to the light; therefore you are preserved, for a time. I think you are beginning to understand that when a positive and not a negative snowman faces the light the result may mean death. Is that why you are afraid to look high in the sky?"

"But I am only a snowman. Why should I be concerned about death? It happens only to people—to old women and to Grammar School girls attacked by lorries. Yet I confess that I am afraid. It is strange that people do not last, that they change, not as snowmen change with their flesh peeling from their body and being replaced with new snowfall but a change which like a touch of iron that has been dipped in burning time and is itself impervious to the force and fury of years, brands the visible human body and no less indelibly the secret individual life which accompanies it. As a snowman, have I thoughts inside my head? What does the inside of my head resemble? Is it like a white barn with rafters, and white mice scampering along the beams and nesting in the corners? What is my head? Is it a stone?"

"Yes, it is a stone. While Rosemary was making you she found a large white stone upon which she packed layers of snowflakes; that is your head. Does it help to know what your head is made of? To know that before the city was conquered by the snowstorm your head stood bald and white on top of a gatepost? Your head was a decoration polished in its circular shape because people admired it that way. It must not make you depressed to learn that your head has been used as an ornament, for it is a custom common among human beings and often persists after their flesh and face and hair and eyes have been added, and no one would guess that a smooth white circular stone was hidden inside.

"I cannot tell you the exact moment when you were born, Snowman. I cannot say, When your right hand was made, then you became a snowman. Or, As soon as your stone head was covered with flakes, then you were a snowman. Or that you have been living since Rosemary had the idea of making you. It is the habit of people to look at the beginning of life in order to determine the moment of birth, but as a Perpetual Snowflake I am not so prejudiced, I know that seed is shed also at the moment of death, and that many people are still not born although they possess bodies with limbs in place and heads with thoughts in place.

"Look at the gap in the sky! It is the sun!"

8.

When I looked up at the sky I could see nothing. Yet I felt my body shuddering and the familiar tears ran down my cheeks, and then in a sudden gust of wind something whirled about me, up and down, then out the gate, onto the pavement, into the pool of black blood, then toward me again, round and round my feet and then up to my head where flip-flop-flap it settled and the gust of wind vanished. I was grateful for the shelter upon my head because I was afraid to look too long at the sky in case I saw the sun, though I scarcely knew how I should recognize it.

"My head is protected now. I have shelter. I cannot even see the sky now."

"You are not the only one to seek shelter from a newspaper; it is common practice. People use it to protect themselves from the weather, others use it to hide from history or time or any of those inconvenient abstractions which man would destroy if only they had a visible shape for him to seize and defeat. Oh these abstractions, Snowman, they are among the most intrusive companions. They are never satisfied unless they have built a nest on the tip of a man's tongue, in the keys of his typewriter, in the hollow of his pen-nib—all favorite places for abstractions to breed and overpopulate the world of words. Even in my talking to you I cannot help mentioning them. Time, I say. Time, History, change. But Time is surely not an abstraction, I think he is a senile creature who is blind because his eyes have been gouged out by an historic fire; his flesh is covered with fur and he licks the hours and swallows them and they form a choking ball inside him. Then Time dies. Time. Death. It is no use, Snowman. The proper place for abstractions is in a region of the mind which must be entered in nakedness of thought. Certain abstractions are powerful and may be lethal yet the way to approach them is not to carry weapons of personification but to act as soldiers do when they surrender, to discard all the known means of defense and retaliation and walk naked toward the hostile territory. Surprising things may happen then, Snowman. We may see abstractions in their truth.

"Truth, death, time, it is no use. How grateful I am that we are made of snow! People need to burn off the old words in the way that a farmer destroys the virgin bush to put the land to new use with controlled sowing and harvesting. I will not say, though, that all such farmers are successful. Their enthusiasm wanes, the crops fail, noxious weeds take the place of the former harmless ones, there are downpours, droughts. And there are always the earliest settlers who yearn for the time when the land was covered with familiar bush and the streams were not dammed to create inexplicable hydro works, and the tall known trees were starred with centuries-old white clematis. But Snowman, Snowman, perhaps words do not matter when it is only a question of surviving for one season. Then the word *Help* is vocabulary enough. Snowmen and Perpetual Snowflakes have no need of words. Snowman, Snowman, look at the gap in the sky. It is the sun."

"I can see nothing while I wear this torn newspaper over my head. I can see only words in print as you have explained to me. Not *help help,* but said Mrs. Frank Wilkinson in charge of the unit I suppose they have seen some deaf and dumb people on buses and in the street and felt sorry that nobody could talk to them the boys admitted breaking into a prefab for food my girlfriend is a nurse and he made her stand in the snow waiting for me to come home before he would let her in made as new suspects arson her behavior seemed quite out of character the role of the church is to provide this not to bribe them into attending they want real religion choice of two modern suites for happy holidays licensed bar dancing not guilty are you hard of hearing you lovers' dream home gas death two sides to him you've had your last chance I'm going to sentence you snowdrops are flowering and crocuses are showing in some places so get ready for spring planting if digging hasn't been done get it over quickly leave large lumps for the weather to work on we can still expect frost and snow fire destroys home heater blaze carpet linoleum were destroyed he woke to the smell of burning planned with you in mind luxury in the sun on the sands by the sea the summer of your dreams stretch black threads or the new nylon web over primula or polyanthus buds before the birds get at them planting can start soon for fruit trees fruit bushes roses he'd finished his lunch when someone rang to tell him it's your shop on fire an unknown young boy discovered the fire he was walking past the shop when he thought he saw smoke or steam in the window monster sale end of season. . . ."

I was beginning to wish that I did not know how to read my newspaper shelter. It seemed full of references to fire and sun and spring, and I thought it strange that human beings should also be afraid of fire and sun and spring, so afraid that they had to keep writing of them in newspapers in order to dilute their fear. Two sides to him? What did it mean? And the picture of the sun puzzled me. I could see the caption clearly—FOLLOW THE SUN—and at first I was foolish enough to believe that if I looked at a picture of the sun it would have the same effect upon me as if I looked at the sun itself. The sun was portrayed as a semicircle with tentacles growing from it, and a wide smiling mouth. What had I been afraid of? So this was the sun, the picture of benevolence; it had not even eyes to see me. Perhaps the smile was too wide giving its face a suggestion of falseness but there seemed to be no doubt about the sun's kind nature.

"Do these newspaper shelters often happen to snowmen?"
"You are a fool of course. As self-centered as any human being. You imagine that newspapers are printed to shelter you from the sun."

"I don't need shelter from the sun. I have seen its kind face."

"It is worse, Snowman, when you are deceived by your own deceit. Newspapers do make convenient shelters for snowmen; also for cooked fish, dog-meat, and they are useful as blankets for tramps; they protect people from the hot and cold weather; they deaden sound; they are the body and tail of kites, and are made into little dishes with flour-and-water paste; they are the heads of puppets, the bed for the cat to have kittens on; they are wrappers, concealers, warmers; also they bring news, even from Rome, Paris, Marseilles.

"Now a gust of wind is blowing near you, Snowman, and for your sake I hope it does not remove your newspaper shelter for when the sun shines it leans close to the earth and the snow is drawn from the earth like white milk from a white breast and when all the snow has vanished and the sun is satisfied the earth lies dry, wrinkled, folded with a dull brown stain spreading through its skin, but you will never see so much, Snowman, nor the change that follows, it is other seasons."

The gust of wind came near me but it did not blow away my newspaper shelter, and toward evening the tears stopped flowing down my cheeks and a cloud of snow fell from the sky but I could see nothing until a blackbird, going home, stopped to rest on the tree, and seeing me standing forlorn, thin, blind, with the world's news clinging to my stone skull, he flew down and pecked at the newspaper, just a slight stab with his beak, tearing a hole in the paper so that once more I could look at the world with my coal-black pine-forest eye. The blackbird had pierced the word *snowdrops*. When I looked out through the gap in *snowdrops* I could see the blackbird disappearing over the roofs of the buildings and thus I could not ask him whether it was joy or sorrow which had impelled him to stab the chosen word.

Tonight I shall sleep deeply. I feel safe. More snow-armies are arriving upon the earth and all will be as it was on my first day. Snow repairs, cushions, conceals; knives have no blades, mountains have no swords, the yellow earth-cat has white padded claws, and it is people only, those bone-and-flesh scissors snapping in the street, re-fusing the overcoat of snow which their shadows wear, sneaking faithfully beside them, it is people who change and die. People and birds.

There is a sound at my feet. Something has fallen from the sky. It is not a snowflake, it is a blackbird and it is dead, I know, for I have learned the dispositions of death. Its beak is half-open and quite still and no living blackbird has such a thrust of beak unless it is taking food or attacking the enemy. Its feathers are ruffled about its neck, its body is huddled, and no living blackbird has such an appearance except in a tree in the wind and rain and now that the snow-armies have arrived for the night the wind does not blow, the tree is still, and there is no rain—but what is rain? How quickly I have learned to gather the clues of death! The bird's claws have as much grasping power now as loose pieces of string. Death has stolen the black sheen of his feathery overcoat and there are two round white pieces of skin like tiny portholes fitted and closed over his once bright watchful eyes. There is a snowdrop lying beside him; its neck is twisted and a green liquid oozes from the crushed stem.

"Snowman, Snowman, there is a gap in the sky."

My sleep is disturbed tonight. I think I must have dozed several times. My newspaper shelter keeps flapping against my face, it seems to have lodged forever upon my head, and I do not really care to harbor or be protected for too long by stale news two sides to him you've had your last chance I'm going to sentence you snowdrops are flowering and crocuses are showing in some places so get ready for spring an unknown boy discovered the fire he was walking past the shop when he thought he saw smoke or steam in the window nobody could talk to them he felt sorry for them because nobody could talk to them they were deaf and dumb.

Stale news. Yet how can I tell whether news is fresh or stale? When the Perpetual Snowflake talks to me of people he brings centuries-old news that is fresh to me, and the stale news of the prompt arrival of each morning brings with it the excitement of fresh news.

A prowling cat has torn the dead blackbird to pieces and eaten him. It is so dark now. I think I will sleep but I am afraid, why am I afraid, I am only a snowman, your last chance I'm going to sentence you two sides to him snowdrops are flowering and crocuses are showing in some places luxury in the sun on the sand by the sea but we do not defeat the sea for we are driven back to the sky or we stay and become what we have tried to conquer, remembering nothing except our new flowing in and out in and out, sighing for one place, drawn to another, wild with promises to white birds and bright red fish and beaches abandoned then longed for.

"Snowman, Snowman."

Man is simplicity itself. Coal, brass, cloth, wood.

I never dreamed.

9.

I believe the armies of snow have deserted me. There are wars of which I know nothing—the wounded and the dead are lying everywhere yet no reinforcements arrive from the sky which I can almost see if I stare through the tiny hole in my newspaper shelter. The clouds are no longer battleships

"Battleships sail with their crews up and down on the sea and wave golden flags and below deck in the dark places of the ship they fill torpedoes with striped sweets, they press buttons which open snow-white umbrellas above the sea, and certainly it is all most beautiful, Snowman, and artistic, the candy floss of death licked by small boys from the hate and fear blossoming on the tall wooden sticks. Splinter crack, the cost. And the white wood with the sap dried. And the heads of trees hustling rumors out of the long-distance wind on its everlasting runabout ticket got cheap the endless circular limits of life.

"I cannot stare so often now at the clouds but I think I see a streak of red which all knowledgeable people on earth will say is blood from a wound but I cannot tell nor do I know if it is fire I am tired of blood and fire what is it oh what is it? I find that I can scarcely breathe. I wish the reinforcements would arrive. What is the use of conquering the earth with snow if the earth does not stay conquered? Oh there are so many rumors everywhere, there's a gossiping trickle of black blood in the gutter, and through the tiny hole in my newspaper shelter I can see swellings on the twigs and branches of this tree. It must be suffering from a disease; perhaps it is dying. People, birds, trees, everything on earth seems to die. I suppose that before many days have passed everyone in the street will have died and how strange it is to think that I have not yet been told about everyone, that they will die and I shall not have known them, and it will not matter because I am only a snowman. But are knowing and being known the two triumphs which the dead carry with them to their graves, the dead who drop like parachutists to the darkness of memory and survive there because they are buckled and strapped to the white imperishable strength of having known and been known, of having made the leap to darkness surrounded and carried by the woven threads of people whom they greeted, abused, loved, murdered, or heard news from even at a great distance, a voice speaking from Rome, Paris, Marseilles or from the forbidden interior where the ticking sawdust desert is wound and whirled and as you have said, Perpetual Snowflake, men die of thirst with their mouth an O like a spokeless wheel full of the dust and sand and red earth, while tall cactus palms extend their greeting and parry at the sky as if they wore great spiked green boxing-gloves in the whirlwind."

"There's little more to tell you, Snowman, of the people in the street of the city. You are only a snowman. It is all the same story, in the end. Widows have husbands living, the spinsters are married, the childless have borne children. Rosemary is not dead. She still sleeps late in the morning until her mother climbs the stairs to her bedroom on the top floor (decorated in red for her thirteenth birthday). 'Rosemary if you don't get up you'll be late for school.' 'All right, I'm coming, have I got a clean pair of stockings?' 'Yes but hurry.' Kath, Harry and Rosemary still drive together in the polished green car which Harry cleans every weekend by removing the little rubber mats and the covers from the covers from the covers of the car seats, shaking everything up and down as if making signals, but that is absurd for you cannot make signals in that way just as you cannot rid the newspaper of its news by shaking it. Snowman, I am not describing a world where a spell has been cast over people forcing them to stay forever within the same moment of time. You saw Rosemary die. Yet she is alive, she goes to school each day, she still dreams of her University student and his long striped scarf. And yet she is also a member of the docile dead who have not yet learned to rebel.

"The idea of rebellion arises in the dead during the first night when they or their ashes lie in their grave and the rain falls all night upon the earth, and the acceptable dampness and darkness where plants thrust and stir and roots are spread with secret buoyancy and warmth like long hair laid softly upon a pillow, change to an uncomfortable wetness with the earth massed in soaking clods knocking and thudding upon the coffin until the rain leaks through to the padded satin, staining it brown, and the stitches decay in the carefully embroidered red-and-white roses, and the ashes and the body whisper with rain and the flesh sinks to accommodate lakes and seas of rain and to make a home for the fugitive creatures which crawl upon the sea bed and are sometimes as brilliantly colored as earth-flowers; and the pools make rainbows, even in the dark. Or so I believe, Snowman. The first night of rain is the loneliest night the dead will ever endure.

"It is on that night that they rebel, and they never forget their moment of rebellion. They are satisfied no longer to be the calm docile dead with their eyes carefully closed and their hands in an attitude of willing surrender; their toes tied to keep up the orderly lifeless pretense. Rain is terrible, Snowman, the way it affects the dead. A night of ceaseless rain on earth is a night of loneliness for human beings who are alive; they draw their curtains—if they possess curtains, if they possess a home. They huddle together touching skin to skin. Or if they are alone and have no one the rag or dress or shirt which they wear is soaked with rain and clings to their skin; it is a time for clinging and touching. The bare feet sink in the earth and the earth grips them, making a hollow place for them. Birds hide beneath a veranda of leaves, perch on the edge of their nest or sit cozily within it and look out, like early settlers sitting on their homestead porch, at the misty frontier of waterfalls.

"How dark it is, Snowman, when rain falls at night, and how lonely for creatures—beasts and men—who are without shelter! It is worse than cold or thunder and lightning, for though cold cuts the flesh with an ax made of ice, it knows its boundary, it keeps its place in the wound even when it strikes completely through flesh and bone. Thunder and lightning are fearsome to people with homes and people without homes, to those who are loved and those who are unloved, but heartbeats are just as terrifying. What cause have the dead to rebel when their bodies lie night after night in quietness with no sound of knocking, of thunder wanting to get in or heartbeats wanting to get out?

"Until it rains at night. Rain penetrates, the stain of it spreads, it sinks deeper, deeper until it arrives at the dead. But you have never seen rain, Snowman, and as one of the dead Rosemary does not yet know it. Perhaps tomorrow or the next night it may rain, and the rain will continue through the night and Rosemary will lie where she has been buried as one of the dead, and the rain will treat her as earth, making pools in her where little fish swim and insects burrow and skate and new streams form and flow from her body to the clay and back again with circular inclusion flesh clay flesh, and for a while she will submit to the rain, and then suddenly it will be time to rebel both against the living and against her companion dead, and she will rise from her grave and with sympathy for no one but herself and her darkness and loneliness she will teach the living through dreams, nightmares, fantasies, the true discomforts of death."

"I do not understand. Why is not everyone weeping? Although you have told me of some of the people in the street of the city I cannot remember them or distinguish one from the other. I only know they live in colonies and grow to look alike, but you have said that berries live in colonies and that holly leaves are webbed like bats' wings and the berries are drops of blood at their vampire mouth."

"I wish you might be, Snowman, when the news arrives."

"Which news? The news has arrived. You see I am wearing it as a protection against the sky."

"Not every snowman has the privilege of looking through a gap in a snowdrop."

I think I have listened to the Perpetual Snowflake for long enough. Since he spoke of the gap in the sky and the sun I have not trusted him. I have become impatient of his stories of the street of the city, and placed here with my feet growing securely in the earth I have no means of deciding whether he has told me the truth. How do I know there are deserts where men die of thirst? The earth is covered with snow; it shall always be covered with snow.

Who is the Perpetual Snowflake? Who is he?

"The wind from the south is blowing and you are disturbed by it, but soon, Snowman, you must have the courage to look up in the sky. There is news of other seasons."

I wait for the night to come bringing more snow, more and more snow to cover the bare places in the street and on the buildings. The snow has melted from the tree, there is a cancer upon the branches, small swellings that will burst and cause the tree to die. The world is gloom and doom where the only survivors are snowmen. Our limbs are not afflicted with cancers from which burst tiny spears of green disease; our life is not a running sore of sap sealing our eyes and ears from the reality behind the deception. Even though stray newspapers force our gaze to pierce the word and not the perilous flower, we learn enough of life in the street of the city to wish that we were wholly snow, that no one had ever called us Snow-Man.

Even my own creator is dead and her father runs back and forth with his polished earphones trying to get in touch with foreign places but no one listens to him for he cannot make the correct signal. I pity the dead and the living people who possess the gift of sight and hearing and are forbidden to use them, who are born to dance but must be propelled from restricting wall to wall in wheelchairs of their own making. Surely the human eye can see beyond the range of telescopes, and the ear hear the sun growing to the height of day tall against the dark dwarfed hours. I talk of the sun but I do not believe in it. Snow is everlasting. I am a snowman. I feel that tonight and tonight and tonight I shall sleep my deep white sleep surrounded by the calm habitual cold air, soft stirring from corner to corner of the world of the white spiders weaving their webs to shroud the trapped earth forever with snow.

Yet it seems that I may have caught the human habit of deception. Here is a little boy, the Italian Salvatore with hair like black paste. He is out late. I think he is going down to the shops to get some cigarettes for his father and chocolates for his mother and his two small sisters. From the downstairs-front room where they live next door to me there is a noise like a market all day, a sound like bargaining and what pleasant bargains they must be, for everyone laughs and seems happy, and then the little girl cries because it is the end of the world, she can see it coming toward her like a terrible dream and it will not stop although she puts up her hands to protect herself oh oh it is the end of the world my lolly on a stick has dropped from its wrapper. When the father is working as a waiter in the West End Salvatore acts as father. He goes shopping. Now he hurries out the door, slithering in the snow at the edge of the pavement. He looks left and right, waits a long time, then he runs across and as he runs he is flapping his right hand against his backside and his legs are galloping and away he goes to the shops. He is a horse galloping through the snow, faster and faster, driving himself gee-up gee-up, and his black paste hair hangs like a mane over his left eye, and he tosses his head, and he snorts with his nose and mouth wrinkled up; away, away he is galloping. His olive skin steams with sweat, he is driven on and on. Suddenly he stoops to the snow, picks up a handful and clamps it in a cold mass in his mouth, drawing his breath sharply. There is the old woman who sweeps the pavement with her silver broom. She scolds him.

"Don't eat snow. It's dirty, it's only dirty water, you'll catch a disease."

Salvatore thinks, I am eating snow, not dirty water. Besides, I am a horse.

He gives a snort, kicks his legs, taps himself smartly on the rump, and is away flying through the sky.

Five minutes later he is home, outside the window, banging upon the pane, "Mama, Mama," to be taken out of the cold into the warm haggling family market that is golden like oranges and yellow and black like ripe bananas.

As I watch Salvatore I think that perhaps people do live forever, their lives are a precious deception which lasts forever. Who dies then? Do snowmen die?

Although I have waited long this evening the reinforcements have not arrived from the sky. I hear something growing, a commotion of roots; it is a disease affecting the earth. I am a mountain, so strong. I am a lamppost with light burning in my head. I am a dragon. I am only a snowman. Now a wind is stirring the sleeping snow; I try to believe that the white mist created by the wind is the reinforcement of flakes from the sky but unlike human beings I am not practiced in deception. I know that I am surrounded by tired snow disturbed from sleep and bleeding from its wounds of light. I wish I had the belief of Salvatore that what lies about me is clean white snow, the proper food of creatures who gallop and fly through the clouds in the sky, but again I remain undeceived, the old woman with the silver broom has been whispering in my ear.

The wind has suddenly blown away my newspaper shelter. I can see. But it is too dark now and the street lights are switched on and the cats are lifting the lids of the dustbins and prowling secure and magnificent through their world, the narrow whisker-lane with smells sprouting in the hedgerows.

"It is not true, Snowman, that before people die they experience a flashing vision of their whole lives. It is a myth someone has dreamed in order to soothe the living, to give them the longed-for opportunity to repeat their lives without effort, without trying in vain to dredge the few lost keepsakes of their memory that have perhaps sunk too deep to be shifted, that may not ever be recovered when the energies are so weakened and the sight is failing and the ears are about to be stopped with the black wax of darkness, and the claws that grew as weapons upon the hands have dried and snapped and are no use for scratching and scrabbling in the darkness of the pool. There was never room either during life or before death for the salvage of so much memory.

"When a man is dying he is afraid or is suffering pain or faith and his thought is of the room where he lies and of the people near him, of their shapes and the flapping of their clothes against their bodies. He does not waste the precious moments thinking, When I was a child: when I was a child I flew kites of gull-wide span; I bounced a rubber ball and watched the shadow of it moving like gray sun-bound elastic across the pavement, and my hands were long gloves of gray shadow; I fished in streams and followed them to their source; I stayed away from school, secretly, and was surprised that I did not know how to use the enormous day which the sun and I together were taking care of, with a promise to use it fast until its mass had become threadbare and glowing with night; the sun and I hacked at the hours, but only the sun made any impression and I was lost against the size of the time, and was glad to give up my task and go home; yet I remember that I learned too quickly to sharpen the huge ax of my needs and desires, and too soon without the help of the sun I reduced each day to darkness.

"No, Snowman, dying is a time of greed. There is no leisurely arranging of food upon one's plate when the plate is nearly empty and when what lies there may also be out of reach."

"Why do you tell me this? I am tired of death. I am not even sure that I believe that people die, not when I see a small boy changing into a horse, galloping through the snow and flying up into the sky while everyone around him thinks that he is still a small boy; not when he tastes a handful of snow and relishes the freshness of it while the old woman with the purple hat and the blue apron and the silver broom whispers in the ears of everyone that new snow is dirty water."

I have been sleeping and now it is morning. The light is sharper than usual, piercing my coal-black pine-forest eye until it seems to threaten to steal my sight. It is a gorse bush of light, ablaze with golden flowers and thorns dusted with yellow pollen. It is dazzling me, there is a white mist rising from me, the world seems filled with a white glare with the golden bush growing upside down from the sky to meet the earth. Am I only a shadow beneath the sea? Or are the sky, the sea, and the golden bush the shadows of my self? It is all the catkin dust in the world swept into a heap in the sky, it is a golden puffball of cloud trampled on my morning with the dust rising and floating and settling upon the earth and the snow, and blown through the air again into the sky. The world is suddenly too old and walked-upon, it is mildewed with gold, soft with gold moss, it has been out in all weathers for too many days and no one has cared to shelter it.

Now the light is dropping bright and sharp and smooth as yellow acorns. They make no sound on the snow.

For so long the snow has lain, the light has settled and been still, and now here is the sun to skim the cream, the top of the light, and spill it everywhere, and the morning laps it up with the wind and the clouds moving their greedy tongues through the sky. The light pours and spills and the first flies are in the air, gummed with sleep.

Oh, oh the sun, see it is a whirling flypaper with the people like new flies clinging to it and drowsy with its dazzle and the syrupy taste of it. But the sun is poison, why don't they realize that the sun will cause them to die? Now people are saying At last, At last. What do they mean? People are opening their front doors and looking out at the street. They are smiling, they are waving; what are they saying to each other?

"I knew it would be soon, not last week or even yesterday but I had an idea today would be the time, I knew it when I looked at the gap in the sky yesterday. Did you see the gap in the sky, did you look in the sky? It is all finished now isn't it, it has never seemed so long, it seems to have been lying here for months and months when it has only been a few days yet it has seemed so long, I thought it would last forever, the way it kept falling and drifting and no sweeping had any effect upon it, and even the traffic did not seem to shift it, for every morning the cars were white and the street and the pavement were without foot or wheel mark or even the mark of a bird or a cat or dog, or even the sign

of that death, you heard of the death in the street, no marks
only the tracks of the wind that cold wind blowing from
the ice, from the north, is it Greenland or Iceland or Spitz-
bergen, one of those places whose names when you pronounce them are sharp with icicles for consonants and lakes
of blue ice for vowels, is it, is it really, did you say Iceland
is a sunny place, I had always believed, I had always believed, but it must have an Arctic climate it can't have green
fields and warm days and the sun if it is up there within the
Arctic Circle, did you ever read those haunting tales of the
Northern Gods, of Balder the beautiful is dead is dead—
the voice passed like the mournful cry of sunward-sailing
cranes—that's poetry we had poetry at school once or
twice—Faster than fairies faster than witches bridges and
houses hedges and ditches, 'From a Railroad Carriage'—but
it's not, true Iceland's not warm and green, I don't believe
it, look at that little boy at the gate slapping his legs and galloping as if he were a horse. A cocky little chap. Look at
him. Thinks he's a horse. The children won't like it now it's
all over will they? There's been no keeping them inside
even when it's been cold enough to change them into ice-
bergs but the worst is to come we've seen one death a night
or two of frost and the streets will be treacherous, and it
was really so pretty in a way, I used to think so didn't you.
Snowmen and snowballs and tasting it, like eating white
clay or frozen flour and dew mixed, and it tasted of nothing
really, so much of nothing that you could imagine special
flavors to it, only the sweetness sourness bitterness which
you put there yourself. Snow is a responsibility don't
you think? Having no color too; you have to mix your

own colors in it and then it is the most personal weather, it is *you*. We were taught to draw snow at school. We made the gray sky with black and white, Chinese or Ivory white, Indian black, a little water, a wash on white paper and the sky was prepared for the snow to fall but we didn't draw the earth because with the snow there the earth had vanished although sometimes we made threads of grass spiking through the white—didn't snow really taste like grass and roots? And wasn't it always an ingredient of nightmares—don't you remember the times you were lost in a snowstorm in the mountains and the snow was in deep drifts around you and still falling and you were so helpless and so much in despair until you saw the light in the distance, the lantern swaying, and then suddenly your forehead was being licked by the warm tongue of a St. Bernard dog and a flask was being uncorked and thrust between your teeth—don't you remember?"

"Snowman, Snowman, the privacy of snow is the privacy of death. Children do not care. They gallop like horses through the streets and fly into the sky."

While I listen to the people talking I am thinking, It is a great mystery indeed the way they talk of snow, of me. How proud I am! One said, pointing to me, "Look at him, he has been here ever since it started, every day on my way to catch the bus at the corner I have passed him standing there. The Dincer girl made him. Rosemary Dincer. And now she's dead, and look at him standing there as if he will last forever, as if, when all the people in the world are dead, struck down by their own brewed secret weather, the only man remaining will be a snowman. Did you ever play that game at school, where someone shouted *No Man Standing*, and immediately everyone lay on the ground as if dead and the last person to be standing was counted out and dismissed from the game? What if the last person standing turned out to be a snowman? He seems to think he may have that honor or disgrace, just look at him there so proud with his piece of coal for an eye and the brass buttons in a row down his belly. I believe they photographed him but they say it was too late for the Dincer girl to see the photo but then photos are always too late don't you think? I mean they are *after* the moment, and it used to depend on the sun didn't it, the direction of the sun and the shadow when you took the photo but somehow it doesn't seem to matter now, the sun has no real say in it, why, you can take photos inside with those tiny bulbs that burst in a flash and nearly blind you, certainly it is out of fashion to rely on the sun but there it is, look, look, oh I wish I were living in one of those places where oranges grow, I have seen pictures of such places. One day in summer I will go to France for the day, early morning and home at night. One day in summer I will go—somewhere—out of town where the sky is a blue water-race going so fast above me that it makes me dizzy, look, it isn't even blue today yet there's the sun, look up at the sky, at the gap between the clouds. Good-by, Snowman!"

They have passed the gate now. They are walking up and down the street. More people have come out, and some are laughing and some are warning each other of the "treacherous" snow. And all look at me with pity and contempt. Why? Why do they keep saying, One day in Spring, One day in Summer, one day soon . . . ?

I have hunched my shoulders and bowed my head. One of the children passing said, "Look he's a dirty old polar bear, the kind they keep in a cage with a pond made of concrete and the rocks painted blue and white to cheat him into believing they are ice, he's just a dirty polar bear, gosh it must be beaut to be a real polar bear coming up through the ice with a block of iceberg balanced on your nose!"

"That's a seal."

"No it's a polar bear. It's tricks."

"It's a seal."

"Seals are gray."

"There are white ones, covered with snow."

"I mean a polar bear, a real one, diving down under the ice and coming up to do tricks and roaring and growling. With a black nose."

"Look at the snowman! Hey, you've taken his arm!"

"I didn't. It came away in my hand. Like this, see!"

"You've taken the other arm. You'll cop it. It doesn't belong to us."

"But it's no good any more, it's melting. Snowmen don't last forever. I bet if I gave it a big push that would be the end of it."

"You'll cop it if you do. Quick, we'll be in for it if someone catches us."

"Want me to knock off his head? I bet I could first go!"

Fortunately they have decided not to knock off my head and they have gone up the street, with that loitering lumbering walk of small boys—they are more like polar bears than I; perhaps they have changed into polar bears because they keep talking of them and imitating their roars and one put his head in the air with his nose trying to touch the sky. He balances a block of ice upon his nose, and that is a feat which I myself would be proud to accomplish yet all a passer-by can say to him is, "Look where you're going, clumsy, you don't want to get yourself a broken arm or leg," speaking with the certainty which adults seem to possess when they imagine they can divine the wishes of children.

The boy looks contemptuously at the woman who tells him in a sharper tone, "You don't want to land up in hospital."

The little boy is wondering, How does she know I don't? Everybody but me has had a broken arm or leg and been in hospital with dishes of bananas and toffees in colored paper beside them for helping themselves any time, and people from the B.B.C. coming with a microphone Now little man and how old are you, how long have you been in hospital, what's your favorite subject at school and what record would you like us to play for you? Everyone in the world has been in hospital and had played for them "My Old Man's A Dustman He Wears A Dustman's Hat he wears gorblimey trousers and he lives in a Council Flat," or "There's a hole in my bucket dear Henry dear Henry," or "There was an old woman who swallowed a fly oh my she swallowed a fly perhaps she'll die." Everyone in the world except me. And there's this stupid woman telling me I don't want to have a broken arm or leg! Gosh! Some people!

The two boys look at each other and at the woman and to me their thoughts are as clear as this bright light surrounding me.

They stare at the woman and they burst out laughing, saying in unison. "Oh my Oh my she's swallowed a fly, perhaps she'll die!"

They look at each other, mirthfully aghast at the suggestion, "Perhaps she'll die!"

In spite of their laughter echoing merrily around the street, I have an increasing sense of deep gloom. It is fine for the children to be content with being polar bears or horses stabled among the clouds champing the fields of sky, lifting their heads, putting out their tongues, seizing between their teeth a cluster of the million burning straws protruding from the sun. And they are content to break their arms and legs, snap, like striped rock, and to fill the snowy air with sharp menacing cries, being birds now with the quills of their shining black wings digging between their shoulder blades. As yet they are not used to the idea of dying; they have not yet set a place for death at their table in order that it may share their meals, or warmed a hollow in their bed for it to lie there at night with its arm around them, protecting them from the dreams by the living.

But why should I mourn the death of creatures on earth? I am only a snowman. I have no arms to fold across my body or hands to clasp as if in prayer. I am only a snowman. My body seems to be sinking slowly into the earth and I am weeping ceaselessly now and I do not know why, and there is a heaviness upon my shoulders as if an unfamiliar burden had been placed there, but where shall I carry the burden, to whom shall I deliver it, when I cannot move and I am planted forever in this garden? When we flew from the sky we stopped the mouth of the earth, filling it with snow, and all the sound the earth has made has been the distant muffled murmur like streams turning in a long wave of sleep, but now there are sharp subterranean cries, articulate demands which reach up through the snow. The sky, the morning, the light, the sun pay attention. Oh I never heard so much sound in my life, and underneath a hush and white steam rising and blurred creatures moving to and fro, meeting and parting. It seems as if the world were on fire.

Where shall I take my burden? Who has put it upon me? I am only a snowman. I cannot bear the weight for much longer. My body sinks deeper into the earth. I have grown thin with the perplexities of being, of merely standing here in a garden in a street of the city. How much more terrible if I were human, moving, traveling, compelled to catalogue the objects of the world in order that I may have remedies for the distress of living; comparing, creating, destroying; putting all into the picture the birthplace the home the first garden tree house street city. And then to die, to submit to the long night of rain, to become a garden pool reflecting and enclosing the face of darkness.

I am a snowman. My flesh is wasting. If I were wholly human I might deceive myself, I might change to any shape which I cared to name and thus live forever; I might imagine that I am not alone, that I can get in touch with everyone else in the world—in Rome, Paris, Marseilles—although I do not understand the language, although when I tried to learn the alphabet of it I found myself lost among columns and archways of letters with my voice only a small echoless whisper. But I am not wholly human. I am a snowman. Surely I shall live forever!

My flesh is wasting. I cannot deceive myself. I have no treasure-house of time or imagination to provide for my survival after death.

Death? But I am a snowman. I live forever. I am growing thin, I am sinking into the earth, soon I shall be bowed upon my knees. The burden is still upon me driving me deeper to the earth. Another small boy passed me just a moment ago and struck me across the head, knocking off the top of my head, and I begin to be more afraid for my thoughts are exposed to the sun which is probing all my secrets, and a white smoke rises from my head; there's something burning, there is no help for it now, I must influence the sun, I must turn my coal-black pine-forest eye toward the sky, to the widening gap in the clouds, and face the sun. I am brave.

"Do you not think I am brave, Perpetual Snowflake?"

He does not answer. I cannot call in a loud voice for I have no voice. The burden is too much, I cannot bear it, I am down to my knees in the earth, all the creatures arriving in time for spring are piling their luggage upon my shoulders, they think I am a snow-porter, a snow-camel, perhaps it is their responsibilities and not their luggage, or the heaviness of their hearts because they know they shall die whereas I, a snowman, remain forever alive and free.

There is a curtain of fire blowing in a great gale of flame.

The pine forest is burning, the pine cones are crackling and sparkling as they are used to doing only when they are ripe and it is time for them to spill their seeds. I have been so afraid of fire. I did not know that I contained it within the sight of my eyes and that when I gazed upon the sun the dreaded fire would originate from myself, that as a snowman I have been deceiving myself into believing I am made wholly of snow when all my life I have carried fire. Is my burden after all the burden of my own fire?

I am weeping now, my cheeks are touched with a red glow, like blood. People looking at me might imagine that I am human. Am I human? Are all other creatures snowmen?

There is no time to think of it, there is no time. I am going to sleep now, and the wall of the sky is patterned with snowdrops, the complete flower and not the broken word or promise.

"Who are you?"

"I am the Perpetual Snowflake."

"Why do you talk to me? Are you here to explain the world to me because I am only a snowman? I should like to know of the place where I am to live for ever and ever. Tell me."

I told him. Sometimes I thought of telling him my own story, of when I too was a snowman in a garden in a street in a city, and how I at last faced the sun and was burned by my own fire until all that remained of me was this small Perpetual Snowflake; how another winter came and I watched the children once again making snowmen and flying like horses through the sky. But I kept silent about my life. I do not want to remember the day when I died and yet did not die, for as almost the only snowflake left on that spring morning I whirled suddenly into the air meeting the Perpetual Snowflake who had guided me in my life, and there followed a battle between us two tiny snow-tissues that were so thin the wind could look through us and shadows could signal to each other through our bodies. I survived the battle. I died once yet I survive. I wait for spring, the sun and the snowdrops and the daffodils, with as much fear as when I was a snowman. How is it that I fear death yet I have died? Or is the human deception true, and death is only a dream, it is death that dies?

Oh how I wish now that I had never conquered the earth, for people live on the earth, and animals and birds, and fish live in the sea but we do not defeat the sea for we are driven back to the sky or become what we have tried to conquer, remembering nothing except our new flowing in and out, in and out, sighing for one place, drawn to another, wild with promises to white birds and bright-red fish and beaches abandoned then longed for.

"Snowman, Snowman!"

Man is indeed simplicity. Coal, brass, cloth, wood—I never dreamed.

a night of frost and a morning of mist

After a night of frost and a morning of mist the day is cloudless. The men of the street have gone to work; the women remain, putting out the milk bottles, shaking the door mats, polishing the windows, dusting the window sills.

Early this morning when the sun had begun to shine warm against my window, a blowfly appeared, the first blowfly of spring, swaggering about in his new navy-blue suit, bumping upon the pane, knocking, clamoring. He skated, he buzzed, he walked upside down and sideways with his feet padded with death. He saw me watching him. He saw me reaching for yesterday's newspaper to fold and creep up and swipe him with it, for he knew that I hated him for appearing so boldly on a day which had emerged in such perfection from a night of frost and a morning of mist. He was a tiny but swelling speck that would block the sun and plunge the earth into darkness. I knew. I wielded my newspaper.

"Don't kill me," he said, in that small voice used by insects, animals, furniture, who appear in fairy stories and startle people (the woodcutter, his son, the young man lying on the grassy bank in the wood, the servant girl sweeping the bedrooms of the palace) with their cries, "Don't kill me, Help! Help!" He knew, however, that he lived in a modern age when cries for help are ignored when they are made by creatures whose feet are padded with death. So he decided to impress me with his fame.

"Do you know," he said, "that in the Science Museum there is an entire display devoted to my life cycle, with illustrations, models, comprehensive labels? Often my family and I put on our Sunday best and visit the Museum, and may I say that we are received with pleasure?"

The thought of his fame did not deter me from advancing with my folded newspaper. Again he cried, "Help! Help!" Did anyone hear him, anyone engaged in present-day folklore—the builder on the new housing estate, the old man lying in the park in the sun, the junior sweeping the floor of the Beauty Parlor, the man from the Water Board inspecting the manhole covers in the street, the workmen replacing the broken paving stones, the woman with her canvas bag slung over her shoulders going from door to door distributing Free Offers, coupons for soap, frozen peas and spaghetti—those who traditionally receive the confidence of insects, animals, furniture, growing plants? Did they hear? Were they listening? Do they listen as carefully as the woodcutter used to do, and the servant girl sweeping the bedrooms of the palace?

"Don't kill me, help help!"

I struck the newspaper against the windowpane and the bossy blowfly was dead.

Then I looked out at the almost deserted street, at the early-spring sun shining down on the pavement stones, at the babies lying in their prams outside the houses, at the men digging up the road near the corner, surrounding themselves with bold notices, red flags, lanterns gleaming like rubies. Then outside my own room I glimpsed the tyrant of Grove Hill Road, a heavy-jowled black-and-white tomcat, the father of most of the kittens in Grove Hill Road, who carries in his head maps of dustbins, strategic positions of milk bottles, exact judgments of the height of garden and street wall, gate, and the wired street trees that now have tiny pink buds on them, like dolly mixture. The tom has long black whiskers. He was sitting on the gatepost, licking his paws.

Most of the people in the street have been longing to "put him down," which, I understand, is the expression used to describe the sinking activity of dying, and one must beware when tying a stone of lifelessness around anything to make sure one does not also attach the stone to one's own neck—they say.

No one owns the tom; he just appears, and leaves in each house a curl of black and white kittens sucking at a contented suave queen. His reproductions in color are faultless.

But I leaned out of my window. "Scat!" I said to the tom, hissing at him. "Go on, scat."

He winked at me.

"First the blowfly, now me," he said. "If the evidence of death does not satisfy you, and the evidence of life satisfies you still less, how in the world are you ever to find satisfaction?"

"Mark my words, you will go to war, my lady."

"Certainly I will go to war," I replied sharply.

And I shut the window and drew a boundary of war, and there I remain to this day, fighting off the armies of life and death which emerge, with the sun, from a night of frost and a morning of mist.

a windy day

When the wind blows in this way the cars bedded in the streets struggle to get free of their green-and-gray canvas or plastic nightshirts; the planes, the new type with their wings down over their hips, rock in the sky. The wind lifts the lids of the dustbins, breaks milk bottles, turns newspapers over and over, around corners, and buffets city sparrows perched in the pruned gray trees.

Spring enters on every gust of wind.

Look at the pearl-colored sky, the satin clouds ruffled this way and that above the chimney tops! The sun is fresh, never left standing or sour, poured out clean on the stones for the dusty-throated wind to lick.

Trains rattle under dark sagging bridges. People talk from pavement to pavement. Children unwind hair ribbons. The black-and-white tomcat slinks along the crumbling wall.

The motorcyclist, his knees tight against his mount, surges through the tidal streets, riding a seahorse to the lonely shore.

The wind moans near the eaves of the house, Why-do-you? Why-do-you?

Settled pigeons call with folded gray voices, Tear up the eviction order.

Homeless birds, intruders, cry for the sea and the marsh-land.

The sun burns a transfer of spring on the city.

Do not be afraid of spring.

commodities—beasts and men

Bought, sold, bought. See them herded through the gates of their hill-paddock, afraid, trusting nothing but their mass, moving together, uttering bewilderment, trying to discover, to master and accept the new boundaries of their lives. Panic breaks out. Why can't they settle?

The fence is plain and complex as a bar of daylight. Why do they tear their hide on the barbed wire, make love to fence posts, nuzzling their flanks against the unreceptive manuka?

Still they bellow, boom their strangeness, trail yellow skitter of fear, turn upon one another. Are they men or massive red-and-white cattle?

In time they will establish themselves in their new paddock, they will learn to understand the habits of vegetation, shade, the notions of weather, the whimsicalities of ponds to quench their thirst, the strength, weakness of fences, gates; the enemies, friends, species beyond.

Night. Panic is stilled.

They lie in their chosen corner with the smell of grass, the taste of water on their breath. They gaze at one another, calm in the certainty of their cud, or they lick their great stained leathered bodies that, collapsible, are folded to fit the grass flattened by their separate beasthood.

They sleep together at last. They are safe. Who are not safe when they have learned to read the map of their world?

And tomorrow?

Bought, sold, bought again; scattering and thundering through the narrow gateway, charging at barbed wire, making love to fence posts, turning in terror to devour one another.

Have these commodities, these bartered beasts and men no final home but Death?

the press gang

Many years ago now the Press Gang used to follow me whenever I set foot in the street after the sun had gone down. I do not know why the going down of the sun should have been a signal for the Gang to appear. They carried ropes to bind me, gags to thrust in my mouth to prevent me from screaming, and a sheet of canvas like a shroud to wind about me and carry me along the dark streets until we arrived at the wharf where the ship was waiting. I was to serve aboard this ship for seven years, and another seven years after that, and so on, until my time was up. I had understood that little girls did not serve aboard ship, but I was informed by the Leader of the Press Gang himself that any human being or animal was subject to demand and was searched for each night when the sun had gone down in all the streets of the towns or the countries of the world.

You can be sure they never caught me. Sometimes when I heard muffled screams in the distance and the hurrying feet on the path outside our gate I would go to the front room and lift aside the blind and watch the shadowy figures passing. Seven years at sea! It was in my sleep one night that I met the Leader of the Press Gang himself. He told me about his work and purpose and stressed the fact that being a little girl made no difference to the need for compulsory service.

In the daytime I worried about the Press Gang. They were said to come upon you so suddenly. You never escaped once you had been seized.

The world was an unaccountable place. Why did a strange transformation occur at night when the tar-sealed roads disappeared, the modern buildings toppled, grass grew in the streets, and people walked from door to door crying Bring out your Dead, Bring out your Dead! Black rats crouched in the doorways, bearded wild-eyed men were hanged in the main street of the realm—why did I live in a realm?—for stealing a loaf of bread or an apple. Did the officials know that I stole apples every morning from the cut-glass dish on the counter of the little shop by the bridge? That I picked holes in the new bread on the way home from school? That I bought a pound of best biscuits, putting them down on the bill and saving half to eat by myself, in secret?

I trembled to think what the officials might know.

Also at night the body-snatchers were about, wearing

long cloaks and visiting the opera disguised as phantoms. And the graves in the grassy cemetery over the hill opened to yield their dead who looked surprised, swathed and damp, like papier-mâché.

And always the ships put out to sea, past the breakwater and the lighthouse, moving swiftly clear of the coast toward the dark horizon. And the cargo of doomed little boys and girls was never seen again.

I grew up; that is not unusual; they say it is destined.

Shadowy night you have not altered in dream or substance. Even now as I tremble with terror and stare at my pale face in the glass, I know the Press Gang waits for me, that I must serve another seven years, and another seven, until the three score and ten are concluded, and the ship and the sun go down together, and Death at last subdues the piratical activities indulged in by Life.

visitors from the fields

I am beset by ideas which swarm about me like bees, and crave belief, like honey, from the secret pockets of my mind. I do not know how to yield my belief. It is raining, the bees say, and I know it is raining, for I can see the rain striding through the streets arm in arm with the wind. Spring is near, they say, and I know they speak the truth for I feel my footsteps echo upon the tiled blue-and-white morning, and the tree in the street is raw with buds.

Telephones are working satisfactorily. Water is running freely down the drains; radio reception is clear.

"The day is neither too hot nor too cold," they say, rummaging for my belief.

"I believe you," I reply. "For I know the state of the seasons and the inclination of the weather."

Then "You are changed," they say. "Ten years ago you were a different woman. Not even your skin remains in your possession. Death is flying in with the last sticks and straw in his beak. . . ."

That is enough. I refuse to listen. I guard closely my honey of belief. I ration it carefully. I fold the petals of my mind and sleep, knowing that for once, at least, the bees will not fly back laden to their overlords in the Fields of Time.

the terrible screaming

One night a terrible screaming sounded through the city. It sounded so loudly and piercingly that there was not a soul who did not hear it. Yet when people turned to one another in fear and were about to remark, Did you hear it, that terrible screaming? they changed their minds, thinking, Perhaps it was my imagination, perhaps I have been working too hard or letting my thoughts get the upper hand (one must never work too hard or be dominated by one's thoughts), perhaps if I confess that I heard this terrible screaming others will label me insane, I shall be hidden behind locked doors and sit for the remaining years of my life in a small corner, gazing at the senseless writing on the wall.

Therefore no one confessed to having heard the screaming. Work and play, love and death, continued as usual. Yet the screaming persisted. It sounded day and night in the ears of the people of the city, yet all remained silent concerning it, and talked of other things. Until one day a stranger arrived from a foreign shore. As soon as he arrived in the city he gave a start of horror and exclaimed to the Head of the Welcoming Committee, "What was that? Why, it has not yet ceased! What is it, that terrible screaming? How can you possibly live with it? Does it continue day and night? Oh what sympathy I have for you in this otherwise fair untroubled city!"

The Head of the Welcoming Committee was at a loss. On the one hand the stranger was a Distinguished Person whom it would be impolite to contradict; on the other hand, it would be equally unwise for the Head of the Welcoming Committee to acknowledge the terrible screaming. He decided to risk being thought impolite.

"I hear nothing unusual," he said lightly, trying to suggest that perhaps his thoughts had been elsewhere, and at the same time trying to convey his undivided attention to the concern of the Distinguished Stranger. His task was difficult. The packaging of words with varied intentions is like writing a letter to someone in a foreign land and addressing it to oneself; it never reaches its destination.

The Distinguished Stranger looked confused. "You hear no terrible screaming?"

The Head of the Welcoming Committee turned to his assistant. "Do you perhaps hear some unusual sound?"

The Assistant who had been disturbed by the screaming and had decided that very day to speak out, to refuse to ignore it, now became afraid that perhaps he would lose his job if he mentioned it. He shook his head.

"I hear nothing unusual," he replied firmly.

The Distinguished Stranger looked embarrassed. "Perhaps it is my imagination," he said apologetically. "It is just as well that I have come for a holiday to your beautiful city. I have been working very hard lately."

Then aware once again of the terrible screaming he covered his ears with his hands.

"I fear I am unwell," he said. "I apologize if I am unable to attend the banquet in honor of my arrival."

"We understand completely," said the Head of the Welcoming Committee.

So there was no banquet. The Distinguished Stranger consulted a specialist who admitted him to a private rest home where he could recover from his disturbed state of mind and the persistence in his ears of the terrible screaming.

The Specialist finished examining the Distinguished Stranger. He washed his hands with a slab of hard soap, took off his white coat, and was preparing to go home to his wife when he thought suddenly, Suppose the screaming does exist?

He dismissed the thought. The Rest Home was full, and the fees were high. He enjoyed the comforts of civilization. Yet supposing, just supposing that all the patients united against him, that all the people of the city began to acknowledge the terrible screaming? What would be the result? Would there be complete panic? Was there really safety in numbers where ideas were concerned?

He stopped thinking about the terrible screaming. He climbed into his Jaguar and drove home.

The Head of the Welcoming Committee, disappointed that he could not attend another banquet, yet relieved because he would not be forced to justify another item of public expenditure, also went home to his wife. They dined on a boiled egg, bread and butter and a cup of tea, for they both approved of simple living.

Then he went to their bedroom, took off his striped suit, switched out the light, got into bed with his wife, and enjoyed the illusion of making uncomplicated love.

And outside in the city the terrible screaming continued its separate existence, unacknowledged. For you see its name was Silence. Silence had found its voice.

the training of my tigers

Do you know the secret of my success with my tigers?

When I am training them and they refuse to leap through the burning hoop I do not punish. I provide my tigers with a different hoop. Sometimes they say to me,

"We do not like the shape of our burning hoop."

"We do not like the material of this hoop."

"We object to the color of the flames."

"If only you would change the hoop we could perform exactly what you require of us. You understand that this will enhance your reputation as a circus trainer."

I believe in tolerance, in listening to the other person's point of view, in vanity. I always obey my tigers. They have trained me very successfully. I have changed the structure of the world in order to accommodate their desires.

And that is why at seven o'clock this evening after the summer sun has gone down I shall be blindfolded and led to the scaffold.

I shall be led to the scaffold every night of my life, and though I protest that the shape of it does not suit me, that the timing, the measurement of the inches between myself and death are crude and inconceivable, nothing comes to my rescue.

I ask, "Where are my faithful tigers?"

I see them in the dark. They are gazing through high-powered magnifying glasses, putting the price upon the jewels they have torn from one another's eyes.

the mythmaker's office

"The sun," they said, "is unmentionable. You must never refer to it."

But that ruse did not work. People referred to the sun, wrote poems about it, suffered under it, lying beneath the chariot wheels, and their eyes were pierced by the sapphire needles jabbing in the groove of light. The sun lolled in the sky. The sun twitched like an extra nerve in the mind. And the sunflowers turned their heads, watching the ceremony, like patient ladies at a tennis match.

So that ruse did not work.

But the people in charge persisted, especially the Minister of Mythmaking who sat all day in his empty office beating his head with a gold-mounted stick in order to send up a cloud of ideas from underneath his wall-to-wall carpet of skin. Alas, when the ideas flew up they arrived like motes in other people's eyes and the Minister of Mythmaking as an habitually polite occupier of his ceiling-to-floor glass ministry did not care to remove ideas from the eyes of other people.

Instead, he went outside and threw colored stones against the Office of Mythmaking.

"What are you doing, my good chap?" the Prime Minister asked, on his way to a conference.

"Playing fictional fives," the Minister of Mythmaking replied, after searching for an explanation.

"You would be better occupied," the Prime Minister told him, "in performing the correct duties of your office."

Dazed, shoulders drooping with care, the Minister of Mythmaking returned to his office where once again he sat alone, staring at the big empty room and seeing his face four times in the glass walls. Once more he took his gold-mounted stick and, beating his head, he sent up another cloud of ideas which had a stored musty smell for they had been swept under the carpet years ago and had never been removed or disturbed until now. One idea pierced the Minister in the eye.

"Ah," he said. "Death. Death is unmentionable. Surely that will please all concerned. Death is obscene, unpublishable. We must ban all reference to it, delete the death notices from the newspapers, make it an indecent offense to be seen congregating at funerals, drive Death underground.

"Yes," the Minister of Mythmaking said to himself. "This will surely please the public, the majority, and prove the ultimate value of Democracy. All will co-operate in the denial of Death." Accordingly he drafted an appropriate bill which passed swiftly with averted eyes through the House of Parliament and joined its forbears in the worm-eaten paper territories in paneled rooms.

Death notices disappeared from the newspapers. Periodical raids were carried out by the police upon undertakers' premises and crematoria to ensure that no indecent activities were in progress. Death became relegated to a Resistance Movement, a Black Market, and furtive shovelings on the outskirts of the city.

For people did not stop dying. Although it was now against the law, obscene, subversive, Death remained an intense part of the lives of every inhabitant of the kingdom. In the pubs and clubs after work the citizens gathered to exchange stories which began, "Do you know the one about. . . ?" and which were punctuated with whispered references to Death, the Dead, Cemeteries, Mortuaries. Often you could hear smothered laughter and observe expressions of shame and guilt as ribaldry placed its fear-releasing hand simultaneously upon Death and Conscience. At other times arguments broke out, fights began, the police were called in, and the next day people were summoned to court on charges relating to indecent behavior and language, with the witness for the prosecution exclaiming, "He openly uttered the word . . . the word . . . well I shall write it upon a piece of paper and show it to the learned judge. . . ." And when the judge read the words "Death," "the dead" upon the paper his expression would become severe; he would pronounce the need for a heavy penalty, citizens must learn to behave as normal citizens, and not flout the laws of common decency by referring to Death and the practices of burial. . . .

In books the offending five-letter word was no longer written in full; letters other than the first and last were replaced by dots or a dash. When one writer boldly used the word Death several times, and gave detailed descriptions of the ceremonies attending death and burial, there followed such an outcry that his publishers were prosecuted for issuing an indecent work.

But the prosecutors did not win their case, for witnesses convinced the jury that the references to death and its ceremonies were of unusual beauty and power, and should be read by all citizens.

"In the end," a witness reminded the court, "each one of us is involved in dying, and though we are forbidden by law to acknowledge this, surely it is necessary for us to learn the facts of death and burial?"

"What!" the public in court said. "And corrupt the rising generation!" You should have seen the letters to the paper after the court's decision was made known!

The book in question sold many millions of copies; its relevant passages were marked and thumbed; but people placed it on their bookshelves with its title facing the wall.

Soon, however, the outcry and publicity which attended the case were forgotten and the city of the kingdom reverted to its former habits of secrecy. People died in secret, were buried in secret. At one time there was a wave of righteous public anger (which is a dangerous form of anger) against the existence of buildings such as hospitals which in some ways cater to the indecencies of death and are thus an insult to the pure-minded. So effective had been the work of the Mythmaker's Office that the presence of a hospital, its evil suggestiveness, made one close one's eyes in disgust. Many of the buildings were deliberately burned to the ground, during occasions of night-long uninhibited feasting and revelry where people rejoiced, naked, dancing, making love while the Watch Committee, also naked, but with pencils and notebooks, maintained their vigilance by recording instances of behavior which stated or implied reference to the indecencies of Death.

People found dying in a public place were buried in secrecy and shame. Furtive obscene songs were sung about road accidents, immodesties such as influenza, bronchitis, and the gross facts of the sickroom. Doctors, in spite of their vowed alliance with living, became unmentionable evils, and were forced to advertise in glass cabinets outside tobacconist's and night clubs in the seedier districts of the kingdom.

The avoidance of Death, like the avoidance of all inevitability, overflowed into the surrounding areas of living, like a river laying waste the land which it had formerly nourished and made fertile.

The denial of Death became also a denial of life and growth.

"Well," said the Prime Minister surrounded by last week's wrapped, sliced, crumbling policies, "Well," he said proudly to the Minister of Mythmaking, "you have accomplished your purpose. You have done good work. You may either retire on a substantial pension or take a holiday in the South of France, at the kingdom's expense. We have abolished Death. We are now immortal. Prepare the country for thousands of years of green happiness."

And leaning forward he took a bite of a new policy which had just been delivered to him. It was warm and doughy, with bubbles of air inside to give it lightness.

"New policies, eaten quickly, are indigestible," the Minister of Mythmaking advised, wishing to be of service before he retired to the South of France.

The Prime Minister frowned. "I have remedies," he said coldly. Then he smiled. "Thousands of years of green happiness!"

Yet by the end of that year the whole kingdom except for one man and one woman had committed suicide. Death, birth, life had been abolished. People arrived from the moon, rubbing their hands with glee and sucking lozenges which were laid in rows, in tins, and dusted with sugar.

In a hollow upon dead grass and dead leaves the one human couple left alive on earth said, "Let's make Death."

And the invalid sun opened in the sky, erupting its contagious boils of light, pouring down the golden matter upon the waste places of the earth.

the pleasures of arithmetic

From my window I look upon the windows of at least ten living rooms in each of which there is a television set which grips light in black-and-white body-hold, which fires people in evening suits at a small target behind the eyes where thoughts also land from time to time unharmed cushioning their fall through darkness. Each night in each of these ten living rooms there are ten times how many people watching the same program, receiving news bulletins (the diminutive of bullets), listening to the same music, and in the end thinking the same thoughts, in the end hosts only at the point of a gun to thoughts donated to them by courtesy of the television company.

Each night in ten rooms ten times how many people.

Thoughts molded on the same last bind the wayward

feet, encourage hard dead growths of nothingness, cause bewildering obstinate pain whose only remedy is resection of the mind.

Thoughts in identical clothes—disguised fox wolf mother enemy husband crowd the frontiers, dull suspicion, criticism, my house is yours, I hold no weapons, I sleep in the belly of the fox before I wake in darkness.

Stamped approved thoughts of equal value, interchangeable, serving as passport, reply coupon, income tax return, pension deposit, life insurance.

I dispense myself red-hot behind the grille, POSITION CLOSED.

PLEASE DO NOT ASK FOR CREDIT AS A REFUSAL CAUSES OFFENSE.

But who would offend, who would dare to offend?

Two million times ten rooms, three million times, fifty million times how many people . . .

The sky swipes with the back of its hand, the sun overtakes in the lane of outer darkness . . .

Multiply replenish the earth with thoughts while the deepfreeze control kills quietly.

Arithmetic is a fascinating pleasure.

"So in the end," said the parson, "the Many became One."

"What we need," said the politician, "is Unity."

"Our aim," said the poet, "is like-mindedness."

How wonderful that all have accomplished their aim, that the wilderness has blossomed with plastic lily of the valley, that the sensitive eye, out-trembling dragonfly, cat's whisker, petals exposed to frost, has made its home in how many million times how many living rooms!

I am glad that I learned arithmetic at school—how else could I experience its perils and pleasures?

Take heed. The sky will not turn the other cheek, the strength of the sun is a single strength, do we raid the monastic thought of the moon?

Of course.

Arithmetic takes no account of Progress. We are still walking to and fro emptying the sea with a sieve while Love sleeps at the Pole, his measurements carved from ice.

an interlude in hell

When the stranger arrived at my door at midnight I was naturally wary of letting him in.

"Friend or foe?" I whispered through the small square window which slides open in the door and enables me to study any visitors before I invite them to my home.

The stranger smiled mockingly. "You don't really believe in categories like that, do you?"

I answered No, slipped my secret window into place, removed the chain from the door, drew the bolt, inserted the key in the lock and at last opened the door.

"Come in then," I said.

The stranger took a few paces inside, drew his gun, and shot me dead.

After I had been allowed some time to get used to the

condition of death, I was called upon to account for it. I explained that I had questioned my assassin distinctly about his feelings toward me. I had asked him, Friend or Foe.

"And did you expect him to reply with the Truth?" my inquisitor asked.

"Yes," I said.

"But he questioned your belief in categories? Friend or Foe. Wet or Dry. True or False."

"Well I am dead," I replied. And I asked for permission to return to earth.

Permission was granted.

So I returned to my former life. And one night at midnight a stranger again arrived at my door and asked to be let in. Again I was naturally wary. I had also grown cunning. I opened the small square window which enables me to view the outside world in safety, and without waiting to ask Friend or Foe I drew my gun and shot the stranger between the eyes. I unhooked the chain, drew the bolt, inserted the key in the lock, opened the door and looked down upon the dying stranger.

"I was your friend," he said.

I wrapped him in a blanket and threw him outside to the three wolves who were waiting in the forest, their six eyes gleaming through the leaves.

These incidents occurred in Hell where I have my permanent home, where the sun strikes while the iron is hot, where Truth becomes a shriveled nothing.

the red-currant bush, the black-currant bush, the gooseberry bush, the African thorn hedge, and the garden gate who was once the head of an iron bedstead

Once upon a time the red-currant bush, the black-currant bush, the gooseberry bush, the African thorn hedge, and the garden gate who was once the head of an iron bedstead lived in a garden. Every morning when the sun rose it shone first upon the other side of the garden where few bushes grew—only clumps of grass, and a hawthorn hedge which used to utter phrases of contempt to her brother hedge who was forced to spend so many hours in the shade with its leaves still damp with dew and its branches cold to the touch.

One day the African thorn hedge whose thorns and red berries were said to be poisonous went into conference with the gooseberry bush, the black-currant bush, the red-currant bush, to try to decide how they could persuade the sun to rise in the west, in order that they should be the first to receive its light and warmth each day. The garden gate who was once the head of an iron bedstead was admitted to the conference because he was a natural eavesdropper and adviser.

How does one persuade the sun to rise in the west and set in the east?

"It is an indisputable fact," the garden gate said, "that the sun must always rise in the east."

"Always?" inquired the gooseberry bush.

"Always. We are faced with the principle of an indisputable fact."

"We must deny it," said the African thorn hedge. "Deny it, overthrow it."

"You cannot overthrow a fact," the garden gate replied. "It has a system of balance which prevents it from toppling, even when it is taken by surprise."

"Forget about facts," the gooseberry bush urged. "How can we persuade the sun to rise in the west? You know that for so many hours each day we stand shivering, cold and damp in the shade. We must think of a plan."

"Don't forget," the red-currant bush said, "the sun has a lifelong habit of rising in the east. It is very difficult to break a habit."

"Ah," put in the garden gate, "But what is the cause of the habit? What led the sun to adopt such an inconvenient habit? Perhaps if we learn more of the sun's behavior and history we may be able to change its ways by gentle persuasion. I have studied, you know," the garden gate added with pride. "As the head of an iron bedstead I found many opportunities for study."

All were silent then, in deep thought, but none could devise a plan. Deadlock was reached in the conference, although not all of the five realized it was deadlock until the garden gate, with his facility for crystallizing atmospheres and moments, announced to them as they sat frowning, silent, chewing inwardly at their leaves, "We have reached Deadlock."

The African thorn hedge looked pleased.

"Thank goodness," he said, "we have arrived somewhere."

"Yes," the others agreed. "We are certainly making progress even if we have only reached Deadlock."

"Oh," sighed the red-currant bush who was something of a dreamer, and whose fruit in the autumn was the most beautiful transparent crimson, "Oh I have always longed to travel! And now we are at Deadlock. Is it a city with towers and tall buildings? Is it a lake? A mountain? Or is it a pool where we have all gathered merely to stare at our reflections in the water?"

"It's just Deadlock," the garden gate answered with some impatience. "It doesn't do to romanticize. Deadlock. Nothing more, nothing less."

It was indeed thoughtless of the sun to spoil their lives by rising in the east and setting in the west. Even now, although the five had been in conference for many hours, the sun's rays had not reached them, while on the other side of the garden the hawthorn hedge sparkled in the light, flaunting her privilege and priority.

"Perhaps the sun is keeping to a command which it is afraid to disobey?" suggested the African thorn hedge.

"That is a thoughtful remark," the garden gate said enviously.

"There are two sides to my nature," the African thorn hedge replied. "There is a garden seat on the other side of me, where people, that is, human beings, sit and talk. I listen, spiking their conversation with my poisonous thorns." He was very proud of his poisonous thorns.

Garden seats were unknown to the garden gate. He was alarmed. "But surely you don't believe all that you hear from foreigners? All foreigners are liars. They are different from us, anyway, and so are not to be trusted."

The idea of a garden seat had frightened him, but his fear was diminished as soon as he thought of garden seats as foreigners.

"Continue the conference," he announced in a bold voice. He would show them that wisdom belonged to him alone and did not need to be derived from strangers such as garden seats and the human beings who inhabit them.

"Where were we? Ah yes, it seems that the sun may be obeying a law."

"Which law?" the African thorn hedge asked.

"Whose law?" the black-currant bush asked. He was very reserved and did not often give his opinion.

"There is no chance, I suppose," suggested the gooseberry bush, "that the law is just something which cannot at all

140

costs be avoided. Perhaps the sun has absolutely no choice. What are we to do then?"

There was silence once again as the five stood deep in thought which is a stream entered always at one's own risk, with no lifebelts or rescue patrols upon the banks.

The hours passed, still without any solution being reached, and the gooseberry bush, the black-currant bush, the red-currant bush, the African thorn hedge, the garden gate who was once the head of an iron bedstead scarcely noticed that they had received their small share of warmth for the day and that the sun was already sinking in the sky.

"I'm cold," the gooseberry bush said suddenly, shivering. "Frost is about."

The red-currant bush agreed. "The authorities have no control over him. They let him come and go as he pleases in spite of the fact that he is a menace."

"My leaves are quite damp now," the African thorn hedge said. "I shall catch cold."

"I have tiny beads on me, hanging in a chain," said the garden gate. "And you have them too," he said to the red-currant bush, smiling at her.

She blushed. "Yes, I wear my beads at night, and in the early morning, but what is the use if the sun does not make them sparkle by shining on them first thing? Oh please, please garden gate, do think of some way of persuading the sun to rise in the west and set in the east!"

The garden gate, who could seldom resist the pleas of a lovely lady like the red-currant bush, stayed awake all night trying to think of a plan. He saw the hedgehogs and the field mice, and the moths switching on their headlights and dithering around corners of moonlight. He saw the stars in the sky, and Frost in his white cloak making finger-marks on the windowpane of the house and spreading stiffened sheets over the grass, for Frost believes that all things have died and that he must provide them with shrouds, in secrecy and silence, in the night. Once or twice, alone and awake, the garden gate, feeling the touch of Frost upon his shoulders, shivered with fear and foreboding. If only morning would come! Yet he still had found no solution to the problem of the sun's rising.

Where is the sun now? he wondered. I suppose he is in bed now, in an iron bedstead with four brass knobs, and bars at each end. I suppose that during the day his instrument of light is one of the brass knobs, highly polished, which he clanks clanks in the sky casting it in people's eyes and having it bounced back to him by those who fear him so much because he has the security and invincibility of rising forever in the east and setting in the west while the remainder of the world toys in the dark, without compass or direction! No wonder the sun refuses to change his routine!

Then a thought came to the garden gate. Why not persuade his friends to move to the opposite side of the garden?

He dismissed the thought. (Thoughts in such moments arrive as employees and may be given wages for their work or refused admission or arrested and thrown into jail.)

"No," said the garden gate. "The *status quo* must be preserved, at least if changing it is going to cause inconvenience to us. It will be a long trek to the other side of the garden. We shall need supplies, refreshments. Perhaps there are dangers of which we are unaware. No. The sun must be persuaded. We could try propaganda, organize skywriting, advertising, to make rising in the west seem of greater value than rising in the east. We could create in the sun a desperate need to rise in the west. We could intimate that any sun which rises in the east is an outsider, an alien, a misfit, a madman who for his own safety, happiness, prosperity, is advised to alter his habits. Then we could arrange broadcasts, take command of television stations, even have it preached in the churches that rising in the east is a deadly sin. Laws could be passed. The penalty for rising in the east could be execution without appeal."

Then the garden gate sighed as he remembered that he was only a garden gate who had once been the head of an iron bedstead. It is true that he understood many of the customs of human beings, yet he had no power to put these customs into practice. He was just a garden gate, swinging on one hinge; it was night and would soon be morning; and he was without a plan.

Many more days and nights passed, and still no solution was reached. The gooseberry bush and the red-currant bush (who was by now very much in love with the garden gate) and the black-currant bush blossomed and hung rich with fruit. The African thorn hedge put on his uniform of bright-red poisonous berries. And the garden gate (who was by now very much in love with the red-currant bush) grew rustier at the hinges and was filled with an energetic desire to swing to and fro, though it taxed his strength; he was no longer a young garden gate.

And on the opposite side of the garden the hawthorn

hedge made her taunting remarks to her brother African thorn.

"The sun always shines first upon me," she teased. "The birds choose me for building their nests in, more than they choose you. I am growing more and more beautiful each day, while you in your vulgar red uniform with your miserable cluster of plants about you, why, words fail me!"

"Why must we have comparisons?" the African thorn asked. "My berries are twice as deadly as yours, anyway."

"But you can't deny that the sun shines upon me most of the day, and that you and all the friends that surround you are left damp and cold and miserable."

No one attempted to deny that, although in a moment of inspiration the garden gate suggested that perhaps if they all denied in loud voices that the sun rose in the east and set in the west, then the whole world, including the hawthorn hedge, would in the end believe them.

"Then there would be no problem at all," the garden gate concluded.

The others were dubious.

"You are trying to imitate human beings," warned the black-currant bush. "It is dangerous to imitate human beings. As the former head of an iron bedstead you have seen and overheard more than is good for you."

The others pondered.

"Your plan might work with something which is invisible, but how can we deny the habits of such a blatant force as the sun?"

The gooseberry bush suggested, "It is often easier to deny the obvious. . . ."

"We could go blind," the garden gate said thoughtfully. "Why not conceive a plan in which everything in the garden is blinded? Then no one can contradict us when we say the sun is rising in the west. But the question is," he added, grinding his hinges, "are we willing to suffer in order to propagate our beliefs?"

"How wisely you speak!" sighed the red-currant bush.

"It's nothing." The garden gate shrugged modestly. "Don't forget that I was once the head of an iron bedstead, and could tell many tales if I were . . . perhaps . . . called upon. . . ."

He rather fancied himself as an after-dinner and twilight speaker. He glanced with longing at the red-currant bush.

"The question," put in the African thorn hedge who was very anxious to reveal the knowledge he had gained from the garden seat, "is that months, almost years of arguing, of planning and plotting, have not changed the problem: How can we persuade the sun to rise in the west and set in the east? Not one of us, in spite of our fancy ideas and so-called wisdom gathered from former or secret lives (here he glanced coldly at the garden gate) has thought of a plan which can be carried out. If the state of things continues we shall all wither and die with pneumonia and lack of sunlight and other dreadful deficiencies the nature of which you ignorant bushes and garden gates are unaware."

They looked respectfully at the African thorn hedge, and waited for his inevitable bright idea.

Alas, he had no ideas.

"We have reached Deadlock again," said the garden gate.

We do nothing but go in and out of Deadlock," the

gooseberry bush complained. "If we are not careful we shall be asked to pay a toll for irregular exits and entrances."

"Deadlock is an unfathomable territory," the wise black-currant bush remarked. And he stood deep in thought, taking care not to be submerged or carried downstream to the sea.

The others followed his example. There was silence. In leaf and iron bar the thoughts crimped, holldid, variaputed, targetriced, until suddenly the black-currant bush twitched its leaves with excitement.

"Now listen," he said.

His companions leaned toward him, except for the garden gate who was inflexible and adamantine by birth and principle.

"Propaganda is no use," the black-currant bush reminded them.

They nodded agreement.

"And it's no use denying that the sun rises in the east and sets in the west. The thing to do is to set up boundaries which exclude the sun from our territory. We must exist without the sun. Unity is strength."

His companions sent up a faint cheer, and the garden gate played rusted martial music.

"If the sun is excluded, then of what importance is it to us where it rises or sets? We can withdraw entirely from the sun's influence, refusing its admission to our territory, living independent of its light and warmth."

The African thorn hedge, the red-currant bush, the gooseberry bush, and the garden gate listened politely, impressed by the apparent wisdom.

"There's a catch in it somewhere," the garden gate said at last.

"Surprising," the gooseberry bush exclaimed, "when someone who has not been the head of an iron bedstead submits a plan you try to find flaws in it!"

"I know there's a catch in it somewhere," the garden gate repeated. "But I shan't go against the majority vote. After all, we have at least passed Deadlock."

All except the garden gate were so enthusiastic about the plan that they stayed awake all night deciding boundaries. They argued and quarreled, almost coming to blows, until they concluded that the whole garden was their territory and that the sun must be excluded from every corner of it. Then, with their problem apparently solved, they fell into a deep sleep (not as deep or swampy as thought) and did not waken until evening of the next day when, using Frost as a messenger, they sent a communiqué to the sun who was at that moment replacing the four polished bed-knobs which he had juggled all day in the sky, and was making himself comfortable in the iron bedstead, pulling the clouds well up to his neck.

"I have brought you an ultimatum, in a silver dish," Frost told the sun who was loath to be bothered, and was not hungry, as he was just putting on his nightcap of darkness with its planetary tassel.

"Taste it for me," he said, yawning, snuggling into bed and arranging the clouds.

Frost tasted it, and told the sun the flavor of it.

"Well," the sun said. "If they want me to keep away from

the garden I don't mind. I'm overworked as it is, juggling polished bed-knobs across the sky until my arms ache."

"One day," said Frost, sidling up to the sun, "you will have to explain why you perform such antics day after day."

"It's a long story," the sun replied.

Frost stiffened with horror. He did not like long stories. He preferred them short, square, inflexible. Therefore he said good night to the sun, and wrapping his silver cloak about him he journeyed to the earth, visiting the garden, spreading shrouds for the dead, stopping the hearts of a few flowers, writing death-messages in black upon the potato plants, the cherry blossom, the pea vines.

Morning came. Waking first, the garden gate wondered at his sense of peace, and then he remembered two things: he had confessed his love for the red-currant bush, and she had confessed her love for him: there was to be no more dispute, conference, or Deadlock about the fact that the sun rose in the east and set in the west.

Soon the African thorn hedge woke, and the red-currant bush (blushing shyly), the black-currant bush and the gooseberry bush. All felt at peace, and spoke agreeably to one another.

"My tiny blossoms will be in bud soon," the black-currant bush mused. "And then my fruit."

"Mine also," said the red-currant bush.

"And I shall put on my uniform of poisonous berries."

"Unity is strength," said the gooseberry bush suddenly, in a mocking tone.

Then the garden gate looked across to the opposite side of the garden.

"The sun is a long time arriving this morning," he said. "I always find it pleasant in the mornings to consider the play of light upon the grass and the hawthorn hedge."

"I feel cold." The red-currant bush shivered.

"We realize, of course," said the black-currant bush, "now that we are awake and the smarting sleep has been ejected by our eyes, smarting sleep and impossible dreams, that we shall no longer be visited by the sun."

"I knew there was a flaw in our plan," the garden gate said, unable to resist having the last word. "It will not affect me, though."

But he glanced anxiously at the red-currant bush who was still draped with frost.

Many hours or days passed, and none knew whether the time was morning or night, for the garden was now filled perpetually with a swirling gray mist. No blossoms appeared on the currant bushes; the berries on the African thorn hedge withered and died, and dropped to the earth. The garden gate was white with frost. No one came to the garden, except Time, who was in disguise and unacknowledged.

"If only we were back in the old days, going in and out of Deadlock!" the garden gate sighed.

But it was too late for such journeys. Deadlock was closed to visitors.

The currant bushes withered, near death, while Frost waited attentively by with the prepared expensive shroud which he had chosen for them. The African thorn hedge was now blind and speechless and fast losing strength. On the opposite side of the garden the hawthorn hedge who had no share in the plan to exclude the sun had died and was already stiff and white. The hedgehogs, field mice, moths, and a little gray rabbit that had burrowed under the fence from next door, huddled together in the mist, trying to comfort one another, while a big moth, head of a family, held its lantern steady, to give them light and warmth. It seemed as if all hope had gone.

Yet if you walk in that garden today, instead of shrouded bodies of long-withered plants and hedgehogs and insects huddled together in fear and trembling, you will see bushes of fruit—black currants, red currants, gooseberries, and a fine flourishing African thorn hedge in a smart uniform with red poisonous berry-buttons. And at night you will see moths, with their usual flopping confusion, trying to guide the traffic of starlight and owls. You will see peace and contentment in the garden.

Why?

Because the garden gate, alone and frozen in the gray light that was neither day nor darkness, and longing for the sun and its warmth, had carefully, painstakingly, traced his ancestry to the iron bedstead in which the sun sleeps at night. The sun, therefore, in a way, could be said to be related to him, to be a member of his family.

"I cannot exclude from my territory a member of my own family, whether he rises in the east or the west," the garden gate said, stirred with love and loyalty toward the sun.

And he ordered Frost to deliver a new piping-hot ultimatum in a silver dish covered by a silver lid, which the sun found too appetizing to resist.

"Of course I will return to the garden," he assured Frost. "The garden gate believes in Influence. I believe in Expediency. As a member of my family he may be useful to me one day; we have common ancestry; I have loyal feelings toward him. And the sun took off his nightcap and got immediately out of his iron bedstead, practiced a few juggling tricks to see if he retained his skill, and with much clanking of polished brass, he visited the garden, bringing life and warmth and light to the dying plants.

That is the end of the story. I have heard that eventually the garden will be destroyed, but I shall not tell about it here. I feel that I have been too tiresome already, and I ask your apologies, please, and I only hope that you are a distant relative of mine. I am a member of the human family. Are you? Shall our garden be destroyed?

an epidemic

Funerals pass more often these days. I count them as I look from my window, and as I walk to the Co-op to buy my groceries; and when I return I report to headquarters the number of funerals I have seen. I do not take detailed notes because I am not a registered spotter of funerals and because it is not often, except in epidemics, that one has the opportunity of practicing the art. You may say that I should keep notebooks with numbers and times, conditions of wreaths and cortege, appearance of mourners, but I tell you again that I am not a professional spotter of funerals. I cannot guess to which cemetery the hearse is driving, whether the corpse is to be cremated, what price the undertakers have charged for their services.

So the dead have come into the open at last, like rats when their private source of food is denied them. The dead swarm in the streets, kept to a semblance of order by tradition and traffic lights. On other days when there is no recorded epidemic the procession of the dead passes unnoticed, unpaid for, and is no source of profit.

Today, everything is different. I am glad that all available resources of humanity dead and alive are being exploited in the urgent drive for . . .

What did you say was the object of the drive? Do you mean to say that we have been misled into a burst of energy for nothing, that we have been lured by a lifelong deceit?

Tell me, what is the purpose of all the activity?

Is it export trade, boost of production?

Did not the Prime Minister say that all resources must be made available in the current campaign?

I do not understand. I understand nothing. I am so lonely that I count funerals, like precious stones. I feed the rats that have emerged from their hiding place. I seek their trust, and they do trust me, I know that they trust me, but their response is not entirely of gratitude—see my bandaged hands, the scars upon my face, and the part of my head where the skull has been nibbled through by the sharp teeth of this infection of humanity?

Where shall our fear come to rest at last and breed sweetness?

Shall we cling for a few more centuries to the top hat, the polished wood, the stone angels, like swarming bees who cling to objects in the hope that they have found a place to install their destiny, who remain there, murmuring their dreams, until the Stranger arrives with gauze mask and gloves to remove them forever to the legitimate hive of Death?

the daylight and the dust

The Daylight and the Dust were on holiday together with nowhere to go.

"I might swoop and bury," the Dust said.

"I might lie between sheets of morning," the Daylight said.

But they packed a little gold bag and a little gray bag and went on tour to blind and smother.

The faithless Daylight betrayed the Dust. The Dust was pursued by his enemies and driven into exile, and to this day the bones of the dead may or may not lie uncovered in the city.

The Daylight continued his journey alone with his little gold bag. He walked up and down the sky, upside down, like a fly, and if you look in the sky you will see him. His little gold bag is the sun.

The sun is a portmanteau of furnaces, boiling remorse, hot scones, tourist equipment and change of history.

And still the Dust blows homeless, in exile, in hiding, cowers in crevices and shaded hollows, on ledges and stone faces, and in anger tears the privacy from impersonal bones and skulls threaded like identical beads in the jewel case of the dead.

The Dust is Breath. Is not Breath the true and only refugee?

solutions

This is a story which belongs in the very room in which I am typing. I am not haunted by it, but I shall tell it to you. It happened once—twice, thrice?—upon a time.

A young man was so bedeviled by the demands of his body that he decided to rid himself of it completely. Now this worry was not a simple matter of occasional annoyance. As soon as the man sat down to work in the morning—he was a private student working all day at this very table with its green plastic cover, drop ends, two protective cork mats —he would be conscious perhaps of an itch in his back which he would be forced to scratch, or he would feel a pain in his arm or shoulder and be unable to rest until he had shaken himself free of the pain which would then drop to the carpet and lie there powerless and be sucked into the vacuum cleaner on a Thursday morning when the woman came to clean the house.

Sometimes as the pain lay upon the carpet the man would engage it in conversation; there would be a lively exchange of bitterness and wit, with the man assuring his pain that he felt no ill-will toward it but he wished that its family would cease inhabiting his body just as he was beginning work for the day. But the pain was cunning. It gave no message to its family which returned again and again, and when it was successfully disposed of by the vacuum cleaner and the County Council Dustmen and transported to a County Council grave, another family of pain took its place.

"I must get rid of my body," the man thought. "What use is it to me? It interferes with my work, and since my work is concentrated in my head I think I shall get rid of my body and retain only my head."

Ah, what freedom then!

There was another difficulty. As soon as the young man wanted to begin his work in the morning, all the feelings which he preferred to inhabit his head to nourish and revive his thoughts, would decide to pack their picnic lunches for the day, and without asking permission, they would set out on the forbidden route to the shady spot between the man's legs where his penis lived in a little house with a red roof, a knocker on the front door, and two gothic columns at the front gate. And there, in the little house in the woods, with the penis as a sometimes thoughtful, sometimes turbulent host, the man's feelings would unwrap their picnic lunch and enjoy a pleasant feast, often sitting outside in the shade of the two gothic columns. And how ardently the sun shone through the trees, through the leaves, in a red haze of burning!

Now you understand that the man became more and more distressed at the way his body demanded so much attention. It had also to be washed, clothed, warmed, cooled, scratched, rubbed, exercised, rested; and should it suffer the slightest harm, pain, like a dragonfly, would alight at the spot with its valise full of instruments of torture which dragonflies used to carry (once, twice, thrice upon a time) when they were the envoys of genuine dragons.

The man grew more and more depressed. He felt himself becoming bankrupt—with his feelings engaged hour after hour in extravagant parties which took no account of the cost, so that bills mounted and could not be paid, and strange authorities intruded to give orders and confuse the situation. And with so little work being done the man did not know where he would find money for rent and food. Sometimes he was so depressed and alone that he wept. His feelings did not seem to care. Whenever he glanced at the little house in the woods he could see at once that all the lights in the house were blazing; he could hear the boisterous singing at night, and witness the riotous carousing during the day under the melting indiarubber sun.

"What shall I do?" the man cried when he woke one morning feeling tired and discouraged. "Shall I rid myself of my body?"

He decided to rid himself of his body, to keep only his head which, he was convinced, would work faithfully for him once it was set free.

Therefore, the same morning, feeling lighthearted and

singing a gay song, the man sharpened his kitchen knife which he had bought at Woolworth's for two and eleven and which had grown blunt from much use as a peeler of vegetables, spreader of marmalade on toast, cutter of string on mysterious packages from foreign countries, whittler of wood on pencils; and, unfolding a copy of the *Guardian*, the man lay it on the kitchen floor, leaned forward, applied the knife to his throat, and in a moment his head had been cut off and the blood was seeping through the Editorial, Letters to the Editor, and the center news page.

The problem which confronted the man's head now was to get rid of the body, and to clean the blood from the kitchen floor. The head had rolled, its face rather pale with the excitement of its new freedom, as far as the fireplace. Now the man knew of three little mice who lived behind the screen which covered the disused fireplace, and who emerged on expeditions during the night and during the day when they supposed that all the people in the house were at work. The three mice had survived many attempts to kill them. One of the lodgers from upstairs had shaken three little heaps of poisoned cereal on a strip of hardboard in front of the fireplace and had waited in vain for any sign that the mice had been tempted. She did not know that the young man had warned them. He had been in the kitchen one evening making himself a cup of tea, and he was just about to take a slice of bread from his wrapped sliced white loaf when he saw one of the mice sniffing at the poisoned cereal.

"I wouldn't eat it, if I were you," the young man said. "Appearances are deceptive you know. Even I have to be careful with every slice of my wrapped sliced white loaf."

"Why are you warning me?" the little mouse asked. "Don't you want to poison me? I thought everybody wanted to poison little mice like me."

"Don't touch that heap of cereal," the young man said melodramatically.

The mouse was formal. "I am grateful sir," he said, and disappeared.

But naturally the mice were grateful, following the tradition of all rescued animals in fairy stories, and as the young man had indeed been living in a fairy story of despair he had no difficulty now, when he had freed himself from his body, in asking and receiving help from the three mice. They were willing to dispose of the body and to clean the kitchen until the floor was without a trace of blood. In their turn, the mice asked the help of the dustbin downstairs, and because the dustbin had often acted as a gay restaurateur serving delectable suppers to the three mice, and because he did not wish to lose his reputation—for reputations are valuable property and must be stored in a safe place (the dustbin kept his just inside the rim of his gray tin hat) he agreed to come into the house, climb the stairs, remove the body, help to clean away the mess, and put all the refuse and the information concerning it, beneath his tin hat. And all this he accomplished with swiftness and agility which won praise and applause from the three mice. Also, with a kindly impulse, the dustbin carried the man's head to his room and even gave it lessons in flying, for the dustbin lid was a relative of the flying carpet and knew the secrets of flight, and that was why he had been so agile in climbing the stairs and moving in and out of the kitchen.

How patiently he taught the head to fly! He waited so courteously and sympathetically until the art was mastered, and then bidding the head good-by returned downstairs (conscious of his new reputation as a hero), out the back door, to his home in the tiny backyard where he lived in the company of a shelf of plant pots and a string bag of clothes pegs which continually quarreled amongst themselves about who were superior, the plastic clothes pegs or the wooden clothes pegs. These quarrels were all the more bitter because they took place among the older generation of clothes pegs; the younger had forgotten or did not know how to quarrel; they were intermarrying and shared shirt flats on the same clothes line; together they topped the country spaces of blankets, and holidayed near the ski slopes of sheets and pillowcases. . . .

Meanwhile, upstairs, the head was flying rapturously to and fro in the bed-sitting-room, and it continued thus in wild freedom all morning and afternoon.

Once it stopped flying and looked thoughtful. "Am I a man?" it asked itself.

"Or am I a head? I shall call myself a man, for the most important part of me remains."

"I'll have one day free," the man said, "to think things over, and then I'll start my intellectual work with no dictation or interference ever again from my presumptuous imperious body. Oh I feel as if I could fly to the sky and circle the moon; thoughts race through me, eager to be set down upon paper and studied by those who have never had the insight or strategy to rid themselves of their cumbersome bodies. My act has made my brain supreme. I shall work day and night without interruption. . . ."

And on and on the man flew, round and round the room in his dizzy delight. Once he flew to the window and looked out, but fortunately no one in the street saw him or there might have been inquiries. Then in the evening, to his surprise, he began to feel tired.

"It seems that sleep is necessary after all," he said. "But only a wink or two of sleep, and then I daresay I shall wake refreshed."

So he lay down beneath the top blanket of his bed, closed his eyes, and slept a deep sleep, and when he woke next morning his first thought almost set him shouting with exhilaration,

"How wonderful to be free!"

That morning the landlady remarked to her husband, "The man in the upstairs room seems to have gone away. I'm sure he did not come home last night. The room is so quiet. His rent is due this morning, and we need the money. I'll give him a few days' grace, and then if we are not paid we shall have to see about finding a new lodger—for this one doesn't seem to do any work really, does he? I mean any real work where you catch the bus in the morning and come home tired at night with your *Evening News* under your arm, and you are too tired to read it."

Also that morning the woman lodger remarked to the other lodger who lived in the small room upstairs, "The man who shares the kitchen with us has not used his milk— see it's still in the bottle. I was curious and peeped in the door this morning (I was only wondering about the milk, it might go sour, in this heat) and his bed is unruffled, it's not been slept in. Perhaps I should tell the landlady. She likes to know what goes on. He seems to have vanished. There's no sign of him."

"Ah," the man was saying at that very moment as he flew about the room, "I don't need to eat now, yet I am full of vigor and excitement. My former despair has vanished. I will start work as soon as I hear the two lodgers and the landlady and landlord bang the front door as they go out on their way to work."

He heard the two lodgers in the kitchen, washing up their breakfast dishes. He heard the landlady putting her clothes through the spin-drier. He heard the landlord go out and start the car.

Then he heard the front door bang, once, twice, three, four times. The house was quiet at last. The man gave a long sigh of content, and prepared to work.

The house was indeed quiet. In the kitchen the three mice emerged from their hiding place to explore and examine the turn of events, for events are like tiny revolving wheels, and mice like to play with them and bowl them along alleyways of yellow light where dustbins glitter and the hats of dustbins shine with pride in their distant relation, the Magic Carpet. . . .

The three mice pattered around the kitchen, and then curious about their friend who had rid himself of his body, they came—one, two, three—into the man's room where they were surprised to observe, on the green plain of the table, the man resting in an attitude of despair.

"Alas," he was murmuring. "Where are my fingers to grasp my pen or tap my typewriter, and my hand to reach books from the shelf? And who will comb my hair and rub the hair tonic into my scalp? Besides, my head itches, there is wax in my ears, I need to keep clearing my throat; how can I blow my nose with dignity? And as for shaving every morning, why, my beard will grow and grow like clematis upon a rotten tree." Tears trickled from the man's eyes.

The three mice felt very sad. "We could help you," they suggested, "by bringing books to you; but that is all. You need arms, hands, fingers."

"I need much more," the man replied. "Who will listen to my words and love me? And who will want to warm an absent skin or picnic in a deserted house, in darkness, or drink from rivers that have run dry?"

"Still," the man continued, "my thoughts are free. I have sacrificed these comforts for my thoughts. Yet although I am no longer a slave to my body I am even now subject to irritations. My vanity demands that I rub hair tonic into my scalp to postpone my baldness, for baldness comes early to our family. My need for relief demands that I scratch a spot just above my right ear. My training in hygiene insists that I blow my nose with a square white handkerchief which has my name—MAN—embroidered in one corner! Oh if only I could escape from the petty distractions of my head! Then I would indeed do great work, think noble thoughts. Even my head offends me now. If only I did not possess my head, if I could rid myself of it, if I could just keep my brain and the protective shell enclosing it, then surely I could pursue my work in real freedom!"

Then the idea came to him. Why not ask the mice to fetch the knife from the kitchen (they could carry it easily, one taking the blade, the second the handle, the third acting as guide) and remove all parts of my head except the little walnut which is my brain? It could easily be done. If the mice hurry, the man thought, and set my brain free, no one knows what great work I might accomplish even today before the sun goes down!

So the mice offered to help. They performed the cutting operations and once again the dustbin and the dustbin lid agreed to collect and conceal the remains. Then, when the task was finished the mice lay what was left of the head, upon the table, and silently (for the man could not communicate with them any more) they and the dustbin and the dustbin lid went from the room, the mice to their corner by the fireplace, the dustbin to his place beneath the shelf where the pot plants lived and the older generation of plastic clothes pegs and wooden clothes pegs continued their quarrels in the string bag where they lived.

Blind, speechless, deaf, the man lay upon the table beside his blank writing paper, his books, his typewriter. He did not move. No one could have divined his thoughts; he himself could no longer communicate them.

That night when the lodger returned from work she peered into the room, and seeing no one there, she reported the fact to the landlady who only that afternoon had replied to inquiries for a rented room.

"The man must have flitted," the landlady said, opening the door and gazing around the room. "The bed has not been slept in. His luggage is still here. But I think he has flitted because he could not pay his rent. I think he was the type. No regular work. No getting up in the morning to catch the bus and coming home at night with the *Evening News* in his pocket and being too tired to read it."

Then the landlady gave a slight shiver of anticipation. "Now I can come into the room and scour it out, wash the curtains, clean the linoleum and the chair covers, redecorate. I'll move the furniture, too, repair the damages he is sure to have done—look, no casters on the chairs, and the spring of that armchair broken, and the cord hanging from the window, and look at the soot on the window sill!"

Then the landlady glanced at the table and noticed the shriveled remains of the man.

"Just look!" she exclaimed to the lodger. "An old prune left lying around. Eating prunes no doubt while he worked; or pretended to work. Such habits only encourage the mice. No wonder they haven't been tempted by the poison I left out for them if they have been living on tidbits from this man!" And with an expression of disgust the landlady removed the deaf, blind, speechless, wrinkled man, took him downstairs and threw him into the dustbin, and not even the dustbin recognized him, for he could never any more proclaim his identity—Man; nor could he see that he was lying in a dustbin; nor could he feel anything except a roaring, like the sound in an empty shell which houses only the memory of the tide within its walls.

And the next morning when the three mice were up early and down to the dustbin for breakfast, one saw the shriveled man, and not recognizing him, exclaimed, "A prune! I've never tasted prunes, but I can always try." And so the three mice shared the prune, spitting out the hard bits.

"It wasn't bad," they said. "It will do for breakfast."

Then they hurried downstairs to hide while the landlady who was not going to work that day prepared the man's empty room for its new tenant, a clean businessman who would work from nine till five and bring inconvenience upon no one, least of all upon himself.

the man who lost confidence

Believing in their wings as endowed articles of faith the five birds flew above the roof tops, alighting on the chimneys and basking in the self-satisfied breathings of smokeless fuel in the controlled zone.

"Never judge a television picture by its aerial," one said. "The sun is impaled and blood flows in the streets. Fingers are nimble as cherries in the pie-filled eyes of the dreamers."

But the Man Who Lost Confidence did not hear. He was turning and turning in the streets of his desolation. He was attending inquiries into simplicity.

"Hello."

The barbed-wire mine-filled electrocuted greeting.

"Hello."

The precipitate years have their own destination; ants are drawing blueprints of the property.

"Hello."

"Kiss me."

"I love you."

The pop singer clicked his fingers, naming the price, and the sentries at the frontiers of the market raised their weapons against the new enemy.

The Man Who Lost Confidence had no words left. He could not talk. He could not walk. He lay alone in bed at last, turning and turning in the streets of his desolation, trying to name the circuit while the rest of the world bounded up and down stairways and spoke full fat sentences fleshed with nouns and verbs, while adjectives and adverbs, like a collection of daily refuse, filled to the brim the two baskets balanced at each flank of the stubborn little donkey trudging through the slum of Thought.

The Man Who Lost Confidence had names for nothing and no one. The divisions of corner, wall, air, solid, were lost.

"Pop singer freezes," the newspaper said. "Pop singer turns to stone."

The five birds, harvesters of cherries, indexed his fertility; the sun released its extra scoop of light upon the stones.

The pop singer died.

"He did not have what it takes," the newspapers said.

An appropriation of names? A nest egg of conformity? Control of the cost and sale price, profit and loss?

In her television bubble bath the lady smiled, soaping her body with perfume worth ten guineas an ounce. . . .

one must give up

There comes a time when one must give up.

So I have given up.

I have canceled delivery of my newspaper. I have removed the connection from my radio, permanently disabling it. The bailiffs in a journey of blessed misunderstanding have taken away my seventeen-inch Portadyne television set where I could switch to both channels and watch interviewers in swiveling chairs driving discussions like cranes through the studio, panelists cut off in the prime of dissension, ladies embracing meat extract and gas ovens, weathermen playing snakes and ladders (throw the dice, up a ladder, down a green-and-yellow-headed snake) with areas of high and low pressure, clicking pop singers cradled inside their own giant candy initial, biting a slice in their self-hunger when out of sight of the camera—after all, one must consume oneself, in the end—timid newsmen introducing a smoky hiccup of old film, women interviewers with pearls at the throat in the manner of doubts in the mind, wax in the ear, stitch in the side, or wolves at the door.

I have given up.

I am now a maker of my own news and distributer of my own time. I receive news which no one thought to broadcast on radio or film for television or report in the newspapers. I choose for myself once again. It is so long since I knew such freedom. Tight-lipped runners arrive bearing word from far countries—from friends two streets away. The cherry tree is in flower. The crocuses are out. The woman in the opposite house washes away the sins committed upon the crazy pavement where dogs have danced, human feet have shed their burden of dust, soot, guilt collected from pacing up and down at midnight upon selected graves.

The pavement is clean once more. The woman empties her blue polythene bucket, sluicing the waste down the County Council gutter while small boys at the end of the street stop and watch the mesmeric flow of water running downhill, hopefully, to the Great Bight occupied by the fabled sea.

Cars pass: minicars, sports cars with the canvas drawn away from their folded ribs, lorries bearing the titles of their load—Military Pickle, Plastic Toilet Seats, Wonderloaf. In the chemist's, around the corner, people read old bound copies of *Time* and *Life* as they wait for their Lotion, Mixture, Linctus.

The butcher arranges the white trays, pooled with blood, in rows in his window, while the cashier in her question box, puppet theater or cave tries to find the reason for the stains on her white overall, since she never handles the meat and steps quickly through the wilderness of sawdust to reach her sanctuary. The thought occurs, Does money cause bloodstains? Have I been knifed in secret by weapons disguised as coins?

In the grocer's the icing on the twopenny-halfpenny torpedo buns slowly melts with the warmth of the oilstove burning in the corner. Stacked upon the top shelf the rusting tins of unpopular food lean, like aged acrobats, their punched-in bellies turned to the light, their proclamations faded to torn wrinkled banners circling their bodies. Some, marked down in price, wonderful value, wear no labels, no news.

The jet unwinds its cotton in the sky where the old-women clouds thread their needles of light, facing the sun, and sew by hand the new bridal dresses for their daughters who are marrying the brothers Rain. Wearing dark suits, with rainbow rosettes in their buttonholes, the grooms will lead their brides to earth, honeymooning in puddles and lakes, making mirrors of each other, returning by sunbeam to the sky where the old-women clouds sit at the door, rumbling their pearly gossip.

The crippled sun chain smokes in a wheel chair striped red and gold. . . .

Fact or fancy. There comes a time when one must rely upon one's own news, images, interpretations, when one must resist the pressure upon one's house of conforming, orthodox, shared seasons, and, using the panel in the secret room, make one's escape to fluid, individual weather; stand alone in the dark listening to the worm knocking three times, the rose resisting, and the inhabited forest of the heart accomplishing its own private moments of growth.

two sheep

Two sheep were traveling to the saleyards. The first sheep knew that after they had been sold their destination was the slaughterhouse at the freezing works. The second sheep did not know of their fate. They were being driven with the rest of the flock along a hot dusty valley road where the surrounding hills leaned in a sun-scorched wilderness of rock, tussock and old rabbit warrens. They moved slowly, for the drover in his trap was in no hurry, and had even taken one of the dogs to sit beside him while the other scrambled from side to side of the flock, guiding them.

"I think," said the first sheep who was aware of their approaching death, "that the sun has never shone so warm on my fleece, nor, from what I see with my small sheep's eye, has the sky seemed so flawless, without seams or tucks or cracks or blemishes."

"You are crazy," said the second sheep who did not know of their approaching death. "The sun is warm, yes, but how hot and dusty and heavy my wool feels! It is a burden to go trotting along this oven shelf. It seems our journey will never end."

"How fresh and juicy the grass appears on the hill!" the first sheep exclaimed. "And not a hawk in the sky!"

"I think," replied the second sheep, "that something has blinded you. Just look up in the sky and see those three hawks waiting to swoop and attack us!"

They trotted on further through the valley road. Now and again the second sheep stumbled.

"I feel so tired," he said. "I wonder how much longer we must walk on and on through this hot dusty valley?"

But the first sheep walked nimbly and his wool felt light upon him as if he had just been shorn. He could have gamboled like a lamb in August.

"I still think," he said, "that today is the most wonderful day I have known. I do not feel that the road is hot and dusty. I do not notice the stones and grit that you complain of. To me the hills have never seemed so green and enticing, the sun has never seemed so warm and comforting. I believe that I could walk through this valley forever, and never feel tired or hungry or thirsty."

"Whatever has come over you?" the second sheep asked crossly. "Here we are, trotting along hour after hour, and soon we shall stand in our pens in the saleyards while the sun leans over us with its branding irons and our overcoats are such a burden that they drag us to the floor of our pen where we are almost trampled to death by the so dainty feet of our fellow sheep. A fine life that is. It would not surprise me if after we are sold we are taken in trucks to the freezing works and killed in cold blood. But," he added, comforting himself, "that is not likely to happen. Oh no, that could never happen! I have it on authority that even when they are trampled by their fellows, sheep do not die. The tales we hear from time to time are but malicious rumors, and those vivid dreams which strike us in the night as we sleep on the sheltered hills, they are but illusions. Do you not agree?" he asked the first sheep.

They were turning now from the valley road, and the saleyards were in sight, while drawn up in the siding on the rusty railway lines, the red trucks stood waiting, spattered inside with sheep and cattle dirt and with white chalk marks, in cipher, on the outside. And still the first sheep did not reveal to his companion that they were being driven to certain death.

When they were jostled inside their pen the first sheep gave an exclamation of delight.

"What a pleasant little house they have let to us! I have never seen such smart red-painted bars, and such four-square corners. And look at the elegant stairway which we will climb to enter those red caravans for our seaside holiday!"

"You make me tired," the second sheep said. "We are standing inside a dirty pen, nothing more, and I cannot move my feet in their nicely polished black shoes but I tread upon the dirt left by sheep which have been imprisoned here before us. In fact I have never been so badly treated in all my life!" And the second sheep began to cry.

Just then a kind elderly sheep jostled through the flock and began to comfort him.

"You have been frightening your companion, I suppose," she said angrily to the first sheep. "You have been telling horrible tales of our fate. Some sheep never know when to keep things to themselves. There was no need to tell your companion the truth, that we are being led to certain death!"

But the first sheep did not answer. He was thinking that the sun had never blessed him with so much warmth, that no crowded pen had ever seemed so comfortable and luxurious. Then suddenly he was taken by surprise and hustled out a little gate and up the ramp into the waiting truck, and suddenly too the sun shone in its true colors, battering him about the head with gigantic burning bars, while the hawks congregated above, sizzling the sky with their wings, and a pall of dust clung to the barren used-up hills, and everywhere was commotion, pushing, struggling, bleating, trampling.

"This must be death," he thought, and he began to struggle and cry out.

The second sheep, having at last learned that he would meet his fate at the freezing works, stood unperturbed now in the truck with his nose against the wall and his eyes looking through the slits.

"You are right," he said to the first sheep. "The hill has never seemed so green, the sun has never been warmer, and this truck with its neat red walls is a mansion where I would happily spend the rest of my days."

But the first sheep did not answer. He had seen the approach of death. He could hide from it no longer. He had given up the struggle and was lying exhausted in a corner of the truck. And when the truck arrived at its destination, the freezing works, the man whose duty it was to unload the sheep noticed the first lying so still in the corner that he believed it was dead.

"We can't have dead sheep," he said. "How can you kill a dead sheep?"

So he heaved the first sheep out of the door of the truck onto the rusty railway line.

"I'll move it away later," he said to himself. "Meanwhile here goes with this lot."

And while he was so busy moving the flock, the first sheep, recovering, sprang up and trotted away along the line, out the gate of the freezing works, up the road, along another road, until he saw a flock being driven before him.

"I will join the flock," he said. "No one will notice, and I shall be safe."

While the drover was not looking, the first sheep hurried in among the flock and was soon trotting along with them until they came to a hot dusty road through a valley where the hills leaned in a sun-scorched wilderness of rock, tussock, and old rabbit warrens.

By now he was feeling very tired. He spoke for the first time to his new companions.

"What a hot dusty road," he said. "How uncomfortable the heat is, and the sun seems to be striking me for its own burning purposes."

The sheep walking beside him looked surprised.

"It is a wonderful day," he exclaimed. "The sun is

warmer than I have ever known it, the hills glow green with luscious grass, and there is not a hawk in the sky to threaten us!"

"You mean," the first sheep replied slyly, "that you are on your way to the saleyards, and then to the freezing works to be killed."

The other sheep gave a bleat of surprise.

"How did you guess?" he asked.

"Oh," said the first sheep wisely, "I know the code. And because I know the code I shall go around in circles all my life, not knowing whether to think that the hills are bare or whether they are green, whether the hawks are scarce or plentiful, whether the sun is friend or foe. For the rest of my life I shall not speak another word. I shall trot along the hot dusty valleys where the hills are both barren and lush with spring grass."

"What shall I do but keep silent?"

And so it happened, and over and over again the first sheep escaped death, and rejoined the flock of sheep who were traveling to the freezing works. He is still alive today. If you notice him in a flock, being driven along a hot dusty road, you will be able to distinguish him by his timidity, his uncertainty, the frenzied expression in his eyes when he tries, in his condemned silence, to discover whether the sky is at last free from hawks, or whether they circle in twos and threes above him, waiting to kill him.